"Deep in thought?"

His baritone voice rolled over Amari and soaked into her skin, fostering the hair on her arms to rise. She inhaled a breath to gather her thoughts and lifted her head. A small gasp slipped out before she could catch it, and any further attempt to draw air into her lungs ceased over the larger-than-life male consuming her vision.

Wearing tan pants and a white collared shirt, Lord Jaxon Blackthorn sat astride a magnificent black beast, his elbow resting on the saddle horn. His mount shifted, and his body compensated with an easy grace. The suns at his back cast him in a muted glow, accentuating his cheekbones and rugged jawline. A breeze kicked strands of black hair across his face in a wildness that pleased her. The man before her would never be mistaken for a sheep, and her body hummed in appreciation.

"Resting," she gasped out, wondering when her lungs would start working again.

Lord Blackthorn glanced toward the others. "By yourself?"

"I like being alone," she said with a small shrug. Fidgeting under his stare, she would have squirmed out of her skin and fled into the surrounding forest if possible. Running trembling fingers through her hair, she concentrated on keeping her heart from thumping out of her chest.

He followed her movements, and she sizzled inside. Her head wound must be more severe than she thought because no sane woman would be excited over the hungered focus of this predator.

ROGUE DRAGON RISING

....

OUTSIDE THE VEIL
BOOK ONE, PART ONE

BY
TJ SHAW

Forgotten Dreams Publishing, LLC
Laveen, AZ

Rogue Dragon Rising, part one

Cover Art by *Dar at Wicked Smart Designs*

Publishing History
Forgotten Dreams Publishing, LLC, 2018
5045 W. Baseline Road, Suite A105-191
Laveen, AZ 85339

Rogue Dragon Rising, part one by TJ Shaw. -- 1st ed.
Digital ISBNs: 978-1-948175-03-6; 978-1-948175-04-3
Print ISBN: 978-1-948175-05-0

Published in the United States of America

Dedication

To my two beautiful, smart kiddos,
you are my joy and inspiration.
Thanks for just being who you are.
I love you!

Acknowledgments

Thank you to CM Wright who managed to edit *Rogue Dragon Rising* despite health issues, and a special thank you to JoAnn at Twin Tweaks Editing who graciously stepped in and took over the editing process for the entire project to ensure all three books in the trilogy shine.

And to Dar at Wicked Smart Designs, wow! You captured exactly what I envisioned for this story. The covers are beautiful. Thank you.

Contents

CHAPTER 1

CAPTURE

Amari raced through the brush. With a quick glance over her shoulder, she confirmed the horsemen pursued her, and not her sister. At the tree line, she paused and looked back across the meadow, beyond the men thundering her way. The unease in her stomach eased as her sister's vivid red dress disappeared into the forest on the other side, toward the safety of the veil and their homeland.

The men's faces were clearer now—determined, hard, and dangerous. They were the trackers, and she, the prey. One man unfurled a rope and swung the looped end, as a grin spread across his face in an I've-got-you-now expression.

Her shoulders stiffened, and with a quick spin, she plunged into the ancient woods. Her sister's lavender perfume lingered on Amari's clothes, a reminder of whom she protected. The overgrown forest shielded her by forcing her mounted adversaries to navigate around the aged trees, yet even with her agility and speed, their unrelenting persistence closed the gap between them.

Onward she ran. Branches clawed at her body and her lungs screamed for relief, but fear kept her sprinting, ducking, and swerving around the dense vegetation. She jumped over a small rise, lost her footing, and tumbled down a steep ravine before landing with a painful *oomph*.

Scrambling up, Amari raced away from the frustrated curses of the men above, but her foot caught on a root and she stumbled. Righting herself, she leaned against an oak tree to catch her breath.

How had her day gone so awry? She had only followed her sister through the veil to the Other Side to pick berries, juicier from the direct sunlight, and never expected to become the mouse in a very real game of chase.

Shouts from the men drew her attention, signaling they had found another way down. Her veil key slapped against her chest as she pushed away from the tree, and she tucked the lightning bolt medallion beneath her tunic so it wouldn't distract her.

The thick canopy stifled any breeze. Sweat dripped into her eyes and plastered her hair against her neck.

Grateful to have defied Mother's wishes, she welcomed her shorn locks instead of her previously long tresses. Her leg muscles burned, yet she fled deeper into the woods.

They pursued, insistent and resolute. The squeak of leather as the men leaned forward in their saddles filtered to her ears. She burst into a clearing, and the horses surged toward her. Needing the shelter of the woods to escape, she darted for the trees, but a man on a roan cut her off.

Bloody hells!

She swerved, but another horse and rider blocked her path. The men played with her, driving her into an increasingly smaller circle. Their laughter pricked her anger as they pushed her toward the middle of the glade.

How dare they treat a lady of the Hawke Royal Court in such a manner!

With a quick prayer to the Goddess Lady Divine, she locked her legs and stopped.

The man riding the roan jerked on the reins to avoid plowing into her, and his horse screamed, rearing up.

Taking advantage of the distraction, Amari dodged the animal's lashing front hooves and raced for the trees. Anticipation filled her. She might make it.

Rough hands grabbed her blouse. With a savage twist, she pulled free, but her feet tangled in the weeds and she somersaulted down an embankment. Twigs tore her clothes and rocks jabbed her body until her head smacked against a tree trunk, ending her out-of-control descent. Moaning, she rolled onto her back.

The men caught up and stared down at her while their horses frothed at the bit, eager to resume the chase.

The man on the roan cursed. "She damaged herself."

"Do you think she will heal in time for the auction?" asked another man, sitting atop a buckskin.

"With her red hair, she won't fetch much," said the third, who sat astride a black and white paint.

"Then if she dies, she won't be a loss to us," replied the first. "Dedrick, she rides with you."

Dedrick dismounted his paint and reached for her, but Amari recoiled from his hand and pain flashed through her side. The starbursts in her head prevented her from warning him his death by her father's hand would soon follow if he touched her. He tossed her over his mount like a sack of grain, and her head exploded in a brilliant flash of light before blackness consumed her.

CHAPTER 2

A DRAGON APPROACHES

Jaxon hated auctions. He despised the persistent shop owners pushing their goods, and most of all, loathed the influx of people who converged on the village during the weeklong event. As if to confirm his point, a slight man who smelled like an herbivore bumped into his shoulder, instigating a snarl from Jaxon's dragon, the beast who shared his soul and lived within him.

"I'm terribly sorry." The man's face paled, and with a quick bow, he bolted into the crowd.

Crispin laughed beside him. "Jax, why do you insist on torturing yourself if you don't like coming?"

"As lord, I am responsible for those who will be working our lands for the next five years." Jaxon glanced at his sentinel, who seemed genuinely amused by his torment. "And I fear what you and Kip will bring home if I don't monitor your acquisitions."

Crispin's grin widened. "Kip's the one you should worry about, not me."

Jaxon spotted his youngest cadre brother striding ahead of them, surrounded by female shifters. With his dimple-enhanced smile, the blond male seemed perfectly at home among the women. "Kip even attracts herbs," he groused. "Have they no sense of self-preservation?"

Crispin's expression sobered. "Drakaina are so scarce since the plague, maybe a predator-herbivore mating is possible."

Jaxon shook his head. "Our dragons would never accept a weaker mate; possibly another strong predator, but never an herbivore."

Crispin nodded, his sea blue eyes pensive. "I fear you are right. So young Kip might as well have his fun."

Jaxon scanned the crowd, his dragon always searching, and he mentally scolded his foolish beast. They were too settled in their ways for a mate. He'd hardened his heart against finding someone to share his life long ago—the day Father left him behind in a cold, lonely world to follow his mother to the Everlasting. His dragon yowled, and Jaxon smiled over the animal's romantic foolishness.

Closing his mind to the fruitless imaginings of what would never be, he pushed through the crowd toward the staging area where he and his cadre—the men chosen as his personal guard—would peruse prospective shifters vying to have their contract purchased.

Another herbivore brushed against him, spurring a warning growl from his beast and additional chuckles from Crispin.

He sighed. How in dragon spit would he survive the day without killing someone?

CHAPTER 3

MEMORIES LOST

After a man named Dedrick transferred her to another called Dorn, the group Amari had been traveling with for the last three days pulled to a stop beside similar caravans in a vast field on the outskirts of a thriving town. Excitement buzzed in the air, but instead of sharing the enthusiasm, heat rushed up her neck to mix with the humid stickiness enveloping her.

At first, she had ridden in an enclosed wagon due to her injuries, but had soon lost that luxury and been forced to walk with the rest of the group. Nausea churned in her belly as she once again tried to remember her identity and why she was here.

Aside from her first name, she couldn't recall anything about herself.

Where is my family? Do I even have a family?

A painful tug twisted her heart. Maybe she had no one. She stifled a sob. Although her ribs and head still hurt, a sharper twinge at the back of her mind threatened to suffocate her. There had to be someone. She couldn't be alone.

I have to remember so I can return to those I love.

With a slow inhale, she gathered her scattered thoughts and looked around. Wagons speckled the meadow like mushrooms while shopkeepers ringed the outer edge of the chaos, peddling their wares from carts. Temporary pens filled with horses, goats, sheep, and a plethora of other animals also dotted the area. She scanned the mass of people, hoping someone would recognize her.

Although the heat didn't seem to bother anyone else, the bright rays from the twin suns blanketed Amari in an oppressive warmth. She huddled beside an old woman near a spoked wheel, frowning over the people who stared at her as they passed. Some even crossed themselves, as if to ward off evil, when they caught sight of her.

Out of the approximately twenty women in her group, not one had red hair. In fact, none of the women she'd seen so far even displayed a reddish-hue. And no one had a short cut like hers.

Dorn, the leader of their group, galloped toward them on his horse, bellowing for them to form a line.

"The auctioneer comes!" cried out the old woman next to her.

Dorn dismounted and stepped alongside the auctioneer.

The auctioneer wore a striped green vest over a red shirt with puffy sleeves. Short salt-and-pepper hair topped his head, and harsh brown eyes hid behind square-rimmed spectacles. He paused in front of each person, asked a couple of questions, then jotted down the responses in a small, black notebook.

Amari's shoulders knotted when the auctioneer stopped at the elderly woman standing beside her.

He eyed the woman whose gray hair sprawled across her slender shoulders in the tangled abandon of one who no longer cared about her appearance. His lips curved down. "You're too old for servitude."

The woman lifted a haughty eyebrow. "My skills as midwife are unmatched."

He hummed in approval. "Your name and specialty?"

"Sousa Mandro. I'm a Glenhaven, so I'm most familiar with sheep, but occasionally, I assisted grazers from nearby herds too."

"Predators?"

Sousa shrugged. "Birthing a baby is the same, no matter the designation. I have no problem tending hunters."

The auctioneer smiled and scribbled in his binder. "You will be easy to place."

With his nose buried in his notebook, he stepped in front of Amari and glanced up. His mouth fell open in what she could only describe as horror.

Even though she didn't understand what was happening, her heart sank. She attempted a smile, but only accomplished a quick twitch of her lips.

The man looked at Dorn and waved his hand in her direction. "What have you brought me?"

"She's unique," Dorn insisted.

"We'll see," the auctioneer grumbled. "Your designation?" he asked her.

"What do you mean?"

The auctioneer stared at her as if she'd lost her mind. "Are you predator or herbivore?"

Her answer consisted of a slow blink, followed by panic.

"Your animal?" he persisted.

Her unease ratcheted into alarm. She grabbed the lightning bolt medallion on the chain around her neck, willing herself to remember. Fear whorled into frustration. Her past remained blank, as if someone had cleaned a tablet and erased her memories along with the chalk dust.

Afraid to divulge she couldn't remember, she tamped down her anxiety. "Sheep," she whispered and, following Sousa's example, added, "from Glenhaven."

Although what she'd said could be true, a niggling sensation at the back of her mind insisted she had just told a whopper. Sousa's resulting gasp only confirmed Amari's lie, but thankfully the elderly woman held her tongue.

The auctioneer's eyes narrowed. "Although the Glenhaven band contains reputable bloodlines, your red hair marks you as a throwback. Throwbacks are hard to place."

Dorn cupped his chin, his expression thoughtful. "She could be a breeder."

"Lords avoid recessive genes to keep their lines pure."

"She's young. Maybe she can work the fields?"

The auctioneer frowned, accentuating an already dour expression. "She's small. Her frame is so slight she would probably blow over in a hard wind. Is she healthy?"

"Of course," Dorn groused, managing to sound indignant.

Amari interlaced her fingers behind her back to keep from fidgeting, but the knocking in her knees roved upward until her entire body quaked. To quell her fear, she concentrated on the ache stabbing her side with every breath.

"I'll put her in a separate lot."

Dorn rolled his eyes. "Just include her with the sheep."

The auctioneer shook his head and marked his pad. "She could contaminate the whole lot if I place her with the other sheep. Look at her. She let a lamb shear her hair, and she smells." He raised a questioning brow. "Are you sure she's not feral?"

Amari gulped. She would know if she were feral...wouldn't she?

Dorn snarled. "You think I'd risk my reputation and entire load by bringing you a rogue?"

"I won't put her with the others."

Dorn sighed. "Fine."

"'Tis better this way. Now, a lord might pity her enough to accept her." Satisfied, the auctioneer moved down the line, but Dorn hesitated, glowering at her. She held her head high and glared back, refusing to cower.

His eyes widened as if surprised by her response, then he broke eye contact and hurried to catch up with the fast-paced auctioneer.

Weak with relief, she started to shuffle out of line, but Sousa grabbed her arm. "Stand still, child. The lords come."

CHAPTER 4

FIRST MEETING

Jaxon glanced over the crowd, spotting Kip, who had just stopped in front of a shifter. "I fear what has drawn Kip's interest."

"With him, who knows," Crispin answered as they angled toward their cadre brother. They approached the row of shifters and the tart smell of their fear filled Jaxon's nostrils. While his dragon thrilled at their discomfort, he garnered a disapproving look from his sentinel.

"You could at least pretend to be nice," Crispin chided.

"I *am* being nice. My dragon hasn't eaten a single one...yet." Jaxon grinned, displaying his incisors, to which Crispin grunted and shook his head.

Still smiling, Jaxon approached Kip. "What have you found?"

Although farther down the line of servitude hopefuls, Rin—Jaxon's ram master—hustled back to stand beside them. "A throwback," Rin grumbled.

Jaxon and Crispin flanked Kip. Standing shoulder to shoulder, they towered above the trembling shifters.

"Have you ever seen such a color?" Kip asked, a bit awestruck.

Jaxon studied the lithe woman wearing a tattered shirt and riding pants—even her boots had seen better days. No taller than five-nine, she took a small step back and bladed her body to make herself less of a target. While the other shifters stood in an open, flatfooted stance, he wondered if the petite herbivore even realized her defensive posturing. Her eyes remained fixed on her footwear, but he had no doubt she was aware of her surroundings...and of him. As with Kip, her red hair captured his dragon's attention. The strands stuck out in every direction, yet glistened in the light like a sunburst. She lifted her startling green eyes and stared at him. "What's your name?" he asked.

Bloody hells. She inhaled a deep breath. "Amari."

"Where did you get that hair?"

She should have counted to ten before responding. Or better yet, just kept her mouth shut. But she hurt, exhaustion rode her, and she didn't welcome the attention, especially when it kept coming back to her hair and its unruly status. So while anyone with a bit of common sense would have remained quiet, she spoke. "Have you not heard about the birds and bees, my lord?"

The blond burst out laughing. "Yes, Jaxon, surely you know that one?"

A low growl reverberated through the air, encouraging the hair on Amari's arms to stand on end.

"I was talking about her hairstyle," the one named Jaxon spat out.

"It is unusual," agreed the third man, who had blue eyes and wavy, black hair.

"Sirs, it doesn't matter. She's a throwback. We don't want her genetics tainting the flock," said a short, stocky man, wearing a simple tan shirt.

An exacerbated sigh slipped out of her as a saying about "reaching the end of her rope" tickled her brain. Although she couldn't remember the exact words, she refused to be discussed like chattel. Her head throbbed, and with every breath, invisible claws raked up and down her side, not to mention the ripe odor permeating her body. The last thing she needed were four men gawking at her as a reminder of her dreadful appearance.

Her gaze narrowed on the one who had just spoken—the short one, with his shirt open in a wide V, displaying a thatch of curly, brown hair—and her temper loosened her tongue. "You best stop calling me a throwback, little man."

Except for his startled gasp, a sudden hush descended over the group. Complete and total silence blanketed them—no people talking, no crickets singing, no birds chirping...nothing.

Her chest tightened. Maybe the saying about the rope had something to do with hanging herself from it. She clamped her tongue between her teeth and silently recited every curse she knew, which of course she *could* remember. The words had just slipped out. Her pain had to be the reason for her sharp tongue because no proper lady would behave in such a manner. And she was a lady, wasn't she?

Like a twenty-mule team beginning an uphill run, the buildup started slow—deep and rumbling—until their bellows shattered the silence. She looked up and tumbled into a pair of obsidian eyes. Except for the stocky one—whose mouth hung open, and rightfully so—the guffaws spilling from the other three shook their broad shoulders.

"Ah, Rin, she would be perfect for your fold," the blond offered.

"Not in my flock," the stocky one named Rin grumbled. "I'll never accept a throw—"

Rin's voice died in his throat at her warning glare, spurring additional chuckles from the other three. He scowled at the delighted trio standing around him. "Of course, you would find her antics amusing," Rin admonished before turning and disappearing into the crowd.

"I believe you hurt my ram master's feelings," Jaxon told her. His voice grated across his vocal cords as if they didn't get used much, the deep baritone shooting straight to Amari's queasy stomach. His gaze bore into her like an arctic blast, and her concentration faltered, but her mouth refused to yield. "He should have better manners if he wants the respect he thinks he deserves."

Jaxon's brows lifted. "Indeed."

His gleaming, black hair swirled in the breeze while chiseled cheekbones and a rugged jaw almost distracted her from the lush curve of his lips. His lips fascinated her. They were the color of a pale rose, offering the only soft place to land on a body that exuded muscle and sinew beneath a white shirt, topped with a blood-red, velvet cloak.

"What is your full name?" Jaxon repeated.

His voice settled over her like warm molasses, and she belatedly acknowledged that her silence would most likely result in a longer lifespan. Staring into his eyes—which weren't completely black after all—the amber ring encircling his irises contracted, as if warning her she stood in front of a creature capable of killing her without a second thought. Sensing the predator within him, her body quivered. Something inside her stretched, and she grimaced.

Jaxon's nostrils flared. His dragon urged him to lean forward and inhale the feisty shifter's scent. He curled his right hand into a fist and ignored his inquisitive beast.

"Are you hurt?" he asked.

She shook her head, the short strands flopping in the wind. She truly had the most amazing hair. The various shades of red appeared to absorb the suns' rays until her locks glowed like fire.

His dragon nudged his fingers, encouraging him to bury his hand within those flames.

His beast wasn't the only one interested, for both Crispin's and Kip's dragons stirred as well. For some reason, he didn't like their attention. He glanced at Crispin, who shrugged.

"Your name?" His voice dropped an octave, his alpha dragon demanding an answer.

"Amari," she gasped out.

His teeth clicked together. She was playing some sort of game with him. Since both he and his beast didn't know the rules, they did not enjoy being the object of her folly. "Your *surname*," he whispered with the quiet venom of one at the top of the food chain.

Her eyes darted back and forth.

He recognized that look. So did the two dragons beside him. This game they all understood and appreciated—a predator chasing its prey.

"I..." her voice stumbled. "I...don't..."

"Sevenson," volunteered the old woman standing beside her. "She's a Sevenson, from the Glenhaven band."

Giving his curious dragon some freedom, Jaxon stepped close and breathed in Amari's scent. Cinnamon spice drifted through his nostrils and settled in his brain. She didn't smell like an herbivore.

Interesting.

"Are you toying with this dragon?" he murmured in her ear.

She did not like him so near, her self-preservation instinct urging her to move away. Although pressed against a wagon wheel, she could have sidestepped out of his reach. But instead, she squared her shoulders and held her ground. Her entire body quaked, yet she stood before him with her chin thrust forward in defiance. Not normal behavior for a sheep.

Kip snickered at his back. "You're losing your teeth, Jax."

"Especially when a sheep challenges the great Jaxon Blackthorn, instead of cowering at his feet," Crispin added.

Jaxon leaned closer, his mouth a hairsbreadth from the delicious curve of her neck. "Is that what you are? A sheep?"

"Of course she is," the elder female reprimanded. "I delivered her myself."

Jaxon stepped back to stand alongside his men. With a slight bow, he acknowledged the old woman. "And did a fine job."

The elder shifter expelled a small *pfft* and turned away, but Amari continued to stare, again such bold behavior not common for her designation. Something about this spirited lamb fascinated his arrogant beast. Maybe it was her blatant disregard for her welfare, or willingness to stand up for herself that intrigued his animal.

Whatever the reason, both he and his dragon recognized the tasty morsel before him did not fit the typical mold of shifters seeking servitude.

While those like Rin would only look at the surface and mark her as a throwback, he saw beneath her façade. A passion burned inside her, making her special. Both man and beast appreciated unique things, especially when wrapped in an appealing package.

"Ladies." He dipped his chin, then turned away from the most curious sheep with the fiery red hair.

CHAPTER 5

A FATHER'S NIGHTMARE

Selena swept into the room, her evergreen scent filling his nostrils. She padded across the polished tile and linked her arms around his waist. Resting her head on his back, she held him close. Her quiet support calmed his beast. Amari had disappeared four days ago, and they still hadn't found his eldest daughter.

"Any news?" she asked.

Greyson twisted and wrapped his arms around her. His mate's soft edges molded to his body for a perfect fit. With Selena his heartbeat, and his children the air he breathed, he couldn't live without any of them, including the unborn babe inside Selena's womb. Dropping his chin atop her head, his hand skirted beneath her hair and settled on her nape in a possessive hold reserved for him alone. "Nolan will arrive soon to discuss the search. We'll find her."

"I know."

His gracious mate tilted her head, exposing lush, green eyes. Her gaze offered him unwavering faith in his ability to find their daughter. His heart warmed, remembering the first time he held his eldest. He had been so afraid of damaging the precious bundle of arms and legs, a true gift from the goddesses.

Even then, his baby girl hadn't been afraid. Her striking eyes, the same color of his mate's, had stared at him in curiosity before she'd reached out and clutched his finger in an unbreakable hold that had only strengthened with the passing years. His little girl had grown into a strong, smart woman and would find a way to survive. He could bear no other alternative.

"Trinity approaches." Selena's voice faltered. "What if we don't find her before then? She won't know what is happening to her."

"Shhh, Lena." He rubbed her back in gentle circles, the satin gown soft against his callused hands. Although he acknowledged the special connection between mothers and daughters, his bond—an unspoken tie with his eldest—had always been absolute and held a special place in his heart. "We will find her long before transition week."

"Greyson?" a voice called out in his mind on the private path he shared with his sentinel.

"We're in the grand ballroom."

"I'll be there shortly."

He grabbed a lock of Selena's hair and rubbed the vibrant ginger strands between his fingers. "Nolan comes. Do you want me to speak to him alone?"

"No, we'll hear what he says together." She gripped him tighter, and he reciprocated by banding his arms around her. Although petite, the moxie running through his mate's spine acted as a testament to her kind.

Needing her strength, Greyson lifted her chin with his forefinger and solicited her lips. She accepted him in an invitation that still heated his blood, and his tongue swept inside her mouth in a claiming kiss. She clenched his shirt within her fists, and he smiled. His mate might be sweet, but a possessive streak burned within her.

Nolan stepped into the shadows of the room, and Selena pulled out of his arms.

Refusing any distance with his mate, Greyson stepped close and slipped a hand beneath her auburn hair, then focused on his cadre brother.

Dirt coated Nolan's duster, and dark circles rested beneath his ashen eyes. Under different circumstances, Greyson would have chastised Nolan for pushing himself to exhaustion, but Nolan protected the young ones in their nest with the fierceness of their kind, and would continue searching until he found her, no matter the cost. "What say you?" Greyson asked.

Nolan dipped his chin to acknowledge Selena, then addressed Greyson. "We followed her trail and scent into the Shabine Forest where three mounted riders captured her, possibly trackers since the annual auction is near."

Selena gasped, and Greyson casually adjusted his hold by wrapping an arm around her waist. His eyes narrowed, noting the tension in Nolan's shoulders. His sentinel withheld information, probably to protect Selena. Nolan kept silent not out of disrespect, but because of an instinctual need for the males to protect the females of the nest.

"What else, Nolan?" Greyson's astute mate whispered.

Nolan glanced at him for direction, and he nodded.

"They stayed within the woods, hampering our pursuit, and we lost them at the Trane River. Bastaine still searches and I'll rejoin him after this report."

If not for the extraordinary hearing of Greyson's kind, Selena's almost imperceptible moan would have gone unheard. His arm tightened around her. "We'll find her, love, don't worry."

She turned into him and trapped a swath of his shirt in her hand before looking up, the trust in her sea green eyes devastating him. "Trinity will soon be upon us. Amari won't know what to do if her body begins to change."

"The moon won't rise for another three weeks. We'll have her behind the veil before then," he assured.

"Will she feel the awakening?"

Greyson glanced over his mate's head to Nolan's impassive face. "Your shield is strong, Lena. There is a good chance it will hold."

"She's *your* daughter," Selena snapped, her voice vibrating with the first hint of anger. "I doubt any shield will hold once the Trinity moon rises. Stop protecting me, Greyson Hawke."

He enfolded his mate within his embrace and lowered his forehead to hers, shielding her with his larger frame. "Your blood also runs through our daughter's veins."

A small frown marred Selena's porcelain face before she faced his sentinel. "Will she, Nolan? Will she experience the awakening?"

Nolan's eyes darkened. He could have feigned ignorance, but his sentinel would never disrespect Selena in such a manner. "The Hawke bloodline is strong. If your shield doesn't hold, she will definitely feel it...sooner than most."

A small tremor shook Selena's body, but reverberated through Greyson like a thunderbolt. She squeezed his hand, then stepped out of reach. He fought the urge to haul her back into his arms, but his mate wouldn't submit to him in her current agitated state.

"Find her, Nolan," she urged with the quiet desperation of a mother fighting to stay strong.

Nolan squared his shoulders. "We will."

Greyson watched the gentle sway of Selena's hips as she walked toward his sentinel. She cupped Nolan's jaw with a delicate hand. Other than a sudden inhale, his sentinel stood motionless. While another man might have been jealous, Selena's affection for Nolan filled Greyson with pride.

"Eat and rest before you venture to the Other Side again," she commanded.

Nolan opened his mouth to speak, but her glare silenced him. "Nolan Bere, Sentinel to the Hawke Cadre and Royal House," she intoned, quoting his full title for emphasis, "you will do me no good if you get sick. Amari needs you...and I need you too," she added in a softer voice.

Nolan's eyes blazed. "Don't worry, we won't let you down."

A reticent smile crossed her lips. She dropped her hand to Nolan's chest and rested it over his heart before she moved toward the door. "I'm going to lie down."

Greyson's jaw clenched. "I'll be up shortly."

She threw him a stern look, but knew him well enough not to protest.

Although he tended to smother during the early months of pregnancy, when it came to his family, Greyson refused to apologize for his overprotective behavior. Selena slipped from the room, and his gaze remained on the doorway. Instead of drowning in elation over this special time, he could only muster a bittersweet miasma. He looked at Nolan, who returned his stare.

Both unyielding.

Both determined.

With a slight nod, Greyson clasped his hands behind his back and stepped onto the balcony overlooking the elegant Eldian city. A cool breeze beckoned him to ride the currents as he scanned the settlement below. Sweeping white-stoned bridges connected the hamlet in a series of pathways, silver pillars rose in spectacular spirals toward the sky, and shops, adorned with ivory and tiled mosaics, sparkled in the setting suns. Traditional dwellings also nestled in the thick canopy of trees.

His gaze drifted beyond the city confines. Although the beauty of the village always brought him peace, the rugged wilderness called to his beast.

Glancing skyward, the veil glimmered in the evening light. Even from afar, the barrier vibrated with power in undulating shades of white and blue. The Eldian race had erected the majestic shield to protect themselves from intruders—specifically dragon-born.

Nolan stepped beside him in silent camaraderie. The serenity of the city contrasted with the harsh splendor of Greyson's birthplace. In his craziest dreams, he had never imagined falling in love with an Eldian royal and leaving his lands to live by her side.

"Do you miss our homeland?"

Nolan hesitated. "Sometimes, but this is home now."

Greyson smiled. His cadre brothers would always remain loyal. He had chosen them well. "We must find her."

"We will. Don't doubt our ability."

He clasped Nolan's shoulder. "I never have."

With a curt nod, Nolan walked across the balcony, but stopped at the archway leading inside. "Selena is well?"

"She worries for her daughter."

Nolan's slate eyes darkened. "We'll bring Amari back," he vowed.

"Do as Selena requested before you take to the skies. I won't face my mate's wrath because you disobeyed her wishes."

For the first time since his return, Nolan smiled. "To avoid putting you in such a compromising position, I will do as she bids," he said, then disappeared inside.

Greyson faced into the breeze, but could find no comfort in the winds for the lost daughter who owned a piece of his heart.

CHAPTER 6

AUCTION

Sousa chuckled. "Congratulations, child. You've garnered the focus of three dragons."

Amari sagged against the wagon wheel. "I don't want their attention."

"If you had kept quiet, you might have gone unnoticed. But now?" Sousa's eyes glittered. "It's too late for you, dearie. You've roused their dragons, and those beasts are insufferable once their curiosity is engaged."

Amari glanced at her shabby boots. What was wrong with her? All she had to do was keep quiet. That arrogant little troll, Rin, had pushed her buttons...buttons she didn't even know existed.

Sousa's hands settled on her hips. "Why did you claim yourself a sheep from Glenhaven to the auctioneer?"

Amari stared at the stranger, who had just come to her rescue by not exposing her. "I don't remember who I am," she said in a trembling voice.

Sousa's bushy, gray eyebrows rose. "Are you even a sheep?"

Amari shrugged.

"Do you remember anything?"

She shook her head.

"Then why do you seek auction?"

An invisible hand squeezed the air from Amari's lungs. "What is auction?"

Sousa hissed and shuffled closer. "Where we offer ourselves for servitude."

Amari's lips pursed. "Why would people do that?"

Sousa stared at her a moment, then Sousa's demeanor became that of a parent teaching a slow child. "Although most herbivores are content living within their familial bands, some want to experience more of the world, but leaving the protection of our domestic lines can be perilous. So, once a year, we can attend an auction where lords have the option of purchasing our contract. After serving our required years, we are free to live on the lord's lands under his protection."

Amari glanced at the people around her. "Everyone here wants to work for a lord?"

Sousa frowned. "Well, maybe not all of us. Those who have shamed their familial ties and were banished have nowhere else to go. Others have committed crimes, and in order to avoid the stockades, have chosen servitude instead."

A lump lodged in Amari's throat. Could she be a criminal or a disgrace to her family? "Why is it dangerous for people to leave their domestic lines?"

Sousa's dusty-brown eyes gentled. "You really don't remember anything, do you?"

"No." The admission amplified Amari's disquiet.

"Because of rogues," the elder woman whispered.

Following Sousa's example, Amari kept her voice low. "What are rogues?"

"The unfortunate ones who fail to transition during their awakening when their animal appears for the first time. They get stuck mid-shift. The pain caused by their inability to transform drives them insane. They are abominations, seeking only bloodshed and violence. The lords protect us from these creatures." Sousa's expression turned reflective. "You don't even remember if you're a predator or herbivore?"

Fearing her voice, Amari shook her head. Tears pooled in her eyes and threatened to fall.

"There, there child." Sousa's frail arm patted Amari's back with surprising strength. "Don't fret. We all have secrets, I will help you."

Amari's downward spiral leveled out, and she rubbed away the tears. Until she remembered, she would rely on Sousa's kindness.

The hollow echo of a bell drew everyone's attention. Dorn broke from the crowd and commanded everyone to follow, leading them to where other groups were gathering around a raised platform with bleachers. Amari marveled over the lords and ladies congregating in front of the stage. Despite her earlier misgivings, she looked for the dragon shifters in the assembling crowd, but aside from the horrid toad, Rin, couldn't locate the other three.

Like a mother hen fussing over its chicks, Dorn handed everyone a card and ordered those with the same color to stay together. Only she held a black scrap of paper. Sousa enveloped her in a quick hug, then hustled over to the other shifters with blue cards.

Amari inhaled a shaky breath. Although she had ignored the severity of her injuries, she now grudgingly acknowledged a possible bruised rib...or two...and the throbbing in her head had only intensified.

The auctioneer approached the podium and rapped his gavel to gain everyone's attention. Shifters from another trader stepped onto the platform to a cheering crowd, and bidding commenced. Voices shouted from the bleachers in rapid-fire succession, but the auctioneer kept the bidding nobles on track.

Whispers from nearby shifters caught Amari's attention. Although excited about their new adventure, they were nervous over not knowing who their employer would be for the next five years.

Amari watched with a sense of detachment as one group after another climbed the three steps onto the platform. More than once, she scanned the lords and ladies in the stands. All were impeccably dressed in fine silks and velour while servants roamed the aisles, offering food and drink. She told herself curiosity had her looking at the crowd, but a small voice in her head said otherwise.

Why did the intimidating dragon lord with the gravelly voice even interest her? Although a stunning male specimen with brooding eyes, rugged good looks, and a body built on strength and confidence, any sane female would stay away from him. She had noticed his dragon stirring within those black water eyes. Yet, instead of fearing the beast inside the man, she'd longed to run her fingers over his furrowed brow to ease the tension marring his striking face.

She looked down, hoping no one noticed the flush heating her cheeks. Through lowered lashes, she eyed the boisterous lords and ladies. Their frivolity dampened her spirit. She may have forgotten who she was and where she was from, but she didn't belong with them. If they were the swans, then she was the swine. She smelled, her body ached, and she'd lived in the same clothes for days.

"Master Dorn, send up your blues," the auctioneer yelled.

Sousa waved at her before climbing the stairs.

The auctioneer rattled off a brief summary, including Sousa's skills as a healer, and a lord with long, black hair and alert eyes shouted out, "Thirty shills!" Rin the Toad also raised his hand, which fostered a small bidding war until the lord shook his head in defeat, and Rin came out the winner.

Sousa bounded down the stage like someone half her age, and stood in front of Amari. "Make sure to hold your head high, dearie, so they see how special you are."

Amari's eyes misted. Sousa's compassion reminded her of someone, someone precious. If only she could remember.

Seeking courage, she slipped into Sousa's open arms for a reassuring squeeze, then turned for the steps. "And now, our final bid for the day...a black."

CHAPTER 7

WAYLAID

Jaxon blazed a path through the crowd, his cloak billowing behind him, anxious to reach the auction. Herbivores hustled out of his way, giving him and his men a wide berth. He paid no attention to the subtle glances and fear pheromones emanating from the nervous shifters.

Herbs were genetically wired to avoid predators—especially dragon-born. Even other predators understood the hierarchical nature and kept their distance. He had grown used to the isolation, came to expect it.

Since most shifters shied away from him, the young redhead's bold attitude toward him earlier baffled his beast. The little sheep either had a steel spine, or a simple mind. With her sharp tongue, he doubted she possessed the latter.

A small smile creased his lips. A fire raged inside that petite herbivore, matching her hair color.

He shook his head to clear his mind, but his body and dragon refused to let her go. Although an herbivore's submissive nature ultimately would never satisfy the predator within him, Jaxon's persistent beast encouraged him to pursue her.

Crispin approached on Jaxon's right and matched his stride. "Are we in a hurry?"

He threw Crispin a warning glare, which prompted a toothy grin from his first. Jaxon smirked. Without war to keep him hard, he must have softened because at some point during their years together, he had lost control over his sentinel.

Kip now flanked Jaxon on his left. "Well, I am. Rin is purchasing a few sheep shifters for me, and I want to make sure he chooses the right ones."

Crispin's nose crinkled. "How can your beast stomach sleeping with a sheep?"

"Now, now," Kip chastised. "My dragon recognizes a fine woman regardless of her designation. I can't help it if your animals are stuck in the ancient ways."

Crispin snorted. "Our dragons don't play with their food."

"And that's why they are so frustrated. You two need to bed something before you explode."

Jaxon growled at his youngest cadre brother.

Kip's mouth dropped open. "See, what I mean? Man, Jax, you need to get laid."

Jaxon sighed. Somehow, he had lost control over *both* his men.

"Ah, shit," Crispin cursed quietly and slowed down.

Jaxon glanced up and stopped mid-stride. Lord Chadrey Wainright, in a poppycock outfit of billowing green sleeves and flowing silk pants, was barreling their way.

Intent on using Crispin and Kip as a diversion so he could escape the pompous dragon, Jaxon turned...and found neither man behind him. His men had abandoned him to Lord Wainright's tedium. He glanced around, but both had disappeared among the throng of people.

"Cowards," he grumbled to them mentally.

Distant laughter filtered through their link.

"We are simply showing respect by giving two lords the privacy they deserve," Kip said in a teasing tone.

"Maybe this will teach you to stop looking at your feet when you're pouting," Crispin added.

Jaxon's dragon snarled. He never pouted. Although he grudgingly admired the swift disappearance of his cadre, he would be the quicker one next time.

He turned back just as Lord Wainright stopped in front of him and clasped his hand. Jaxon forced a smile, but was already formulating an escape plan.

"Lord Blackthorn, I'm surprised to see you mingling among the masses."

Jaxon dipped his head, displaying the proper greeting of one lord to another. "Auction comes but once a year. I would be remiss not to attend."

Chadrey's ruddy cheeks lifted with his smile. "What are you seeking to purchase?"

"Rin wants to increase the sheep population and a few other herbivore positions," he answered, attempting to pull his hand from the robust man's grip.

"Ah, yes. I hear this is going to be a bountiful year. We'll need to fortify our field workers if we want to capitalize."

Jaxon nodded and again failed to extract his hand from Chadrey's grasp. The elder dragon had the tenacity of a bulldog when he wished to discuss something, but Jaxon had known Chadrey for years, and while the man couldn't be hurried, he could be prodded.

Placing his free hand on Lord Wainright's back, Jaxon encouraged the man forward with a gentle push. "I'd hate to miss the entire auction."

"Oh, of course," Chadrey mumbled, and released Jaxon's hand.

Jaxon glided around the patrons milling among the carts and storefronts with the fluid grace of a predator, but Chadrey tarried.

"So, your nest is still empty? Your dragon must be restless for a mate."

Jaxon's teeth clicked together. *How many times are we going to have this conversation?*

"Drakaina are rare these days," he replied with his usual response.

"True," Chadrey agreed. "That's why I would like to send Lorelai for a visit once you return home."

Jaxon bit his tongue. *Crispin and Kip are dead men when they resurface.*

A three-legged dog scurried by, and Jaxon's dragon whined, eager to be underway. Yet Jaxon refused to acknowledge his desire to attend the auction had anything to do with a certain redheaded sheep.

He noticed Chadrey's inquisitive look and realized the man still waited for a reply. "Lorelai is lovely, but my beast has no interest."

Chadrey continued, undaunted. "A few seasons have passed since you last saw her. She has matured into a fine dragoness and would bring honor to your nest."

"I have no doubt she is beautiful, but my dragon doesn't wish to settle down."

Chadrey's face crumbled. "I understand your beast hopes to find its true mate," he murmured in a voice so low, Jaxon almost couldn't hear it above the buzz of the marketplace. "My dragon searched for countless seasons until we lost hope. Then I met Lorelai's mother."

Jaxon's animal quieted, knowing Chadrey still mourned the loss of his mate. "Marabel was lovely," he said in a soothing tone.

Chadrey nodded, a reminiscent smile touching his face. "She was a remarkable woman," he added before grabbing Jaxon's arm and stopping them in the middle of the thoroughfare. "Although I loved her deeply, as my dragon cherished her drakaina, Marabel wasn't my mate."

An uneasy tension tightened Jaxon's shoulders. "Everyone saw the love between—"

"But she wasn't my *true* mate," Chadrey emphasized. "Sometimes, my young lord, our dragons become so obsessed in their quest for the unobtainable, they fail to see what's right in front of them."

Jaxon rifled a hand through his hair. Although his beast ignored the elder's words, Jaxon couldn't be so dismissive. Drakaina—mature female dragons—were rare. Even though several years had passed since the plague, many young dragonesses still didn't survive to

44

adulthood. Those who did were precious, and more often than not, hidden until maturity to protect them from overzealous suitors.

He glanced beyond the dirt-trampled field to the trees and endless sky above. An alpha dragon lived within him—tough, possessive, and overbearing, but willing to love and sacrifice with all its heart. Although Lorelai would make an excellent mate, both he and his dragon had no desire to court her.

"Lorelai's drakaina is strong and needs a dominant male to tame her," Chadrey said, his eyes clouding. "Her animal will never submit to the young, untested courtiers clamoring for her affection. If her drakaina doesn't yield, she will never produce offspring, and I long to hear the patter of little feet, Lord Blackthorn."

Although a growing disquiet urged Jaxon to abandon Chadrey in the thoroughfare and hurry for the stage, he refused to show such rudeness. "I'm sure she will find someone."

Chadrey's grip on his forearm tightened. "Let her visit," Chadrey pleaded. "Make your dragon look at her. Give Lorelai a chance to prove herself worthy of your alpha."

Jaxon pinched the bridge of his nose with his thumb and forefinger. His arrogant beast wouldn't be pleased, but he could always force a union. Although he had vowed never to take a mate, maybe a wife would ease the lonely nights. Maybe the time had come to stop looking to the skies and focus on the land. "Very well, but I make no promises."

Chadrey grinned. "I understand."

"Now if you will excuse me, I really must be going."

Chadrey raised a brow. "I've never seen you so interested in the auction. Doesn't Rin handle your purchases?"

Not bothering to answer, Jaxon waved farewell and lengthened his stride. Yes, Rin had an aptitude for acquiring suitable shifters, but his ram master had no intention of purchasing the shifter he wanted most.

CHAPTER 8

THROWBACK

Clutching her black card, Amari clambered up the three steps to the center of the platform. Following Sousa's advice, she held her head high, but her resolve crumbled as all eyes turned to her and the conversations from the lords and ladies died away. Even the auctioneer held his tongue.

Mouths fell open and eyes widened as they took her—and all her glorious filth—under consideration.

"What is her designation?" asked the man who had lost the bidding war with Rin.

"Sheep from the reputable Glenhaven band," shouted the auctioneer.

"A throwback?" Murmured whispers.

"Look at her red hair!" Nervous titters.

"Someone sheared it." Bold laughter.

"No wonder the Glenhaven alpha demanded she seek auction."

The sting of their words pierced Amari's defenses like darts through a cotton sheet. She scanned the crowd for a friendly face, but only well-pampered men and women stared back at her. She spotted Rin, and judging by his grin, he appeared pleased over her discomfort. Inhaling a deep breath, she bowed her head. Her body vibrated with the urge to flee, but since she had nowhere to go, she doggedly stared at her boots.

"Do I hear ten shills?" cried out the auctioneer.

Silence.

"Five?"

Crickets.

"Fifty shills," yelled the black-haired man who had lost to Rin.

"Deal!" The auctioneer slammed the gavel before anyone could respond, as if fearing the buyer would recant his offer.

"You're a fool, Nicula," belted an obese lord from the bottom row.

"That's more than an entire lot of sheep," trilled a lady wearing a satin blue gown.

Amari lifted her head and braved the lords and ladies mocking her to look at the man who had bought her contract. His dark eyes appraised her. She would have fidgeted under his scrutiny, except he smiled—a genuine smile, warm and infectious, and meant for her. Aside from Sousa, no one had shown her such kindness. For the first time in days, the knots in her stomach eased. She would find her way...and she would remember.

Her lips tipped in a tentative smile until a sudden hush settled over the lords and ladies as two men approached the platform. Amari recognized the men who stopped beside Rin, sandwiching the little toad between their powerful bodies. While the atmosphere in the crowd chilled, her body warmed— Lord Blackthorn's men had arrived.

Although she couldn't hear their words, a heated exchange seemed to take place, which culminated when the dark-haired one slapped the back of Rin's head.

Rin threw his hands up in exasperation and stepped out of reach.

An instant later, Lord Blackthorn pushed through the lingering crowd. The blond man grabbed Jaxon's forearm and whispered in his ear. Jaxon nodded once, then looked up at her.

Amari's heart stumbled. Something stirred inside her, restless and wanting. Jaxon's midnight gaze refused to release her, and the rest of the world narrowed until only one man filled her vision.

Strands of his black hair blew across his face as a low warning growl rumbled out of him, fostering a mass exodus of the bleachers. His hands clenched into fists at his sides, tightening the corded muscles in his forearms. Raw power radiated from his body, charging the air.

An inner voice encouraged Amari to follow the fleeing nobles, yet she remained, having never witnessed anything more breathtaking. Heat flushed through her body. Lord Blackthorn appeared to be ruled more by his dragon, exuding danger and self-confidence. She should run and rejoice in the fact he hadn't purchased her contract, but instead, she could only stand and stare.

The auctioneer stepped in front of her and grabbed her arm, breaking the spell Lord Blackthorn had woven over her. Another growl rippled through the air, but the auctioneer seemed oblivious to the danger. "Off my stage," he commanded. "Go find your new employer."

The auctioneer then pushed her toward the steps. Still in a daze, she stumbled down the stairs and straight into Sousa's waiting arms.

"Oh, my dear, Lord Nicula Sorin has chosen you!" Sousa leaned back and held her at arm's length. "He's from a fine house and is very protective of his charges. What a grand place to spend your years."

Amari smiled, but searched the dwindling crowd for the dragon who had just scrambled her emotions. Lord Blackthorn and his men had disappeared. Although irrational, disappointment washed over her.

Sousa cupped Amari's chin to gain her attention. A thoughtful expression played across the healer's face. "I hope calling yourself a sheep was a wise decision."

Amari lifted her shoulders in a small shrug and swallowed the lump in her throat. "Since I don't know my animal, and no one seems to be looking for me, I must make my own way until I sort everything out. Claiming myself a sheep has bought me time."

A large bear of a man sauntered toward them and bellowed, "Throwback!"

Sousa whirled on the man with the speed of a viper. "Her name is Amari. Remember it."

The man's eyebrows flew up in surprise, but then he chuckled, his belly jiggling with his shoulders. "Forgive me, healer," he said with a small bow. "Sometimes my manners are not as my mother taught." He turned to Amari and also bowed. "Forgive me, Lady Amari, but Lord Sorin requires I gather up all the new charges. You are the last."

Amari stifled a moan as Sousa's hug compressed her tender ribs.

Standing on tiptoes, Sousa whispered in her ear. "You have a strong spirit; when the time is right, you will remember."

Amari stepped out of Sousa's arms, wiping away a stray tear. "I will always cherish your kindness."

Sousa nodded, her eyes bright. With a small wave goodbye, the only friend Amari could remember walked over to the other sheep still waiting for someone to direct them.

Straightening her shoulders, Amari looked at the bear-man. "I'm ready," she said with more confidence than she felt.

"Name is Shane. I'm the herbivore foreman."

"Pleasure to meet you," she said, and fell in step beside him as he led her away from the stage.

"I'm taking you to the wash tent so you can bathe and put on clean clothes. After that, you'll go to the herbivore tents where you can eat and rest before we leave for Nicula's lair in the morn."

"What is Lord Sorin's...designation?" She bit her bottom lip, hoping the question wasn't too personal.

Shane scowled. "You don't know?"

Amari curled her fingers into her suddenly sweaty palms. "I never paid much attention to matters outside...my flock."

"You are unusual, aren't you?" Shane smiled. "I've never met someone who hadn't researched every lord and lady in advance before applying for auction."

"I like to live on the edge."

He laughed. "You sure you're a sheep?"

Her stomach lurched. Why couldn't she just keep her mouth shut? "Of course," she snapped.

Shane stopped at the opening of a tent near a strand of willow trees. "Seems to me, your temper matches your hair color," he said casually. "Since you were the last auction, the other new charges have already bathed and gone to their assigned tents. Nicula separates herbs from predators so everyone feels comfortable. The boys have emptied all the tubs, except for one, and a clean gown is inside." He pointed to another tent. "A sleeping mat is inside that one, and they're still serving dinner behind it."

She murmured her thanks and hurried inside. Desperate to wash off the grime, she peeled off her clothes and slipped into the tub. The icy water numbed her body, but she took time to lather and rinse her hair. Only after scrubbing herself clean, did she inspect her wounds.

Although the large bump along her hairline had lessened in size, her other injuries were more troubling. With gentle fingers, she probed her ribs.

Several were so sensitive, she could barely touch them, and a dark bruise covered most of her left side.

With a resigned sigh, she stepped out of the tub and dried off, hoping a good night's sleep and some warm food would alleviate her weariness and help her heal faster.

She held the plain white gown in front of her and her nose wrinkled in distaste, but since most of the sheep females wore similar gowns, she reluctantly pulled the cloth over her head and let it slide down her body. Even though she still hurt, the bath and fresh clothes did revitalize her a bit.

After tucking her lightning bolt pendant inside her dress, she stepped out of the tent to find evening shadows had settled upon the land. A cool breeze dried her hair with a vigor that most likely left her looking like a porcupine, but she didn't care because of the most delectable aroma filling her nostrils. Although the traders had fed her greens and various grains, she hadn't had a decent meal in days, and her stomach grumbled over the smell of roasting meat.

She approached the cooking tent, and her knees almost buckled over the savory aroma. Reaching for a plate, she licked her lips in anticipation, but a spoon shot out and smacked her hand.

"Ow!" She snatched her stinging appendage out of harm's way and stared at an elderly woman, who still brandished the wooden weapon with the confidence of one not afraid to use it again.

The woman's gray hair, pulled into a severe bun, accentuated her intimidating glare. "Herbs don't eat with the predators."

Amari sighed. Did it really matter where she ate? If she weren't so hungry, she might have argued with the grumpy food monitor, but instead, she forced a smile and asked where to go.

Using her weapon as a pointer, the woman grumbled, "Over there, with the other herbs."

Amari spun on her heel and headed for the herbivore line, passing several men and women who sat around tables. The men wore baggy cotton pants and white shirts while the women's gowns were identical to hers. Only Amari's red hair kept her from blending in completely with all the other blondes and browns.

Learning her lesson, she waited for the woman on the other side of the food station to smile in welcome before reaching for a plate. Her choices were greens, grains, fruits, and some sort of gruel. Hopes of a warm meal plummeted, along with her appetite.

How do these people survive?

Although disappointed, she still loaded her plate before shuffling off to a nearby table occupied by a blonde-haired mother and her young son. The woman kept her eyes averted, but the boy stared at Amari with the awed interest of youth. "Look at your hair!" he exclaimed.

"Camden," his mother admonished, "leave the lass to her meal and mind your own."

The boy's face crumbled. "Sorry."

Amari smiled at the youngster. "No worries."

The boy looked up, his brown eyes still asking the questions his mother wouldn't allow him to voice. She dragged her fingers through her choppy locks. "Since red makes me easy to find, short helps me run faster."

"How fast?"

"Very," she said with a solemn nod.

"Wow!" He grinned, his eyes sparkling with awe.

"Camden, finish your greens," his mother ordered, though she gave Amari a tentative smile.

Camden nodded and dug into the food on his plate. Amari stared at her dinner with less enthusiasm. Although she did like salads and grains, she longed for something more.

While picking through the various shades of green, reality dawned on her. She was an herbivore and sheep didn't eat meat. For the next five years, the intoxicating aroma of cooking venison would always tease her palate, but never fill her belly.

She pushed her plate away and stared into the darkening shadows beyond the fires. How would she ever fit into this life without her memories? She must have done something so terrible, her family had abandoned her. Tears bubbled to the surface, and though she blinked them away, she couldn't ignore the dull ache in her chest.

"You done?" Camden asked, pointing at her plate.

She glanced across the table to the hopeful boy. "Yes, do you want it?"

Camden looked at his mother for permission. "Are you sure?" the young woman asked.

Amari nodded.

"Thank you," Camden's mother said in an appreciative tone. "You know how growing rams are...always hungry."

Amari stood and offered a small smile. "Have a good night," she said before walking around to the front of the sleeping tent and slipping inside. Locating a thin mat at the back, she laid down. No, she didn't know. She didn't know anything.

CHAPTER 9

MORNING RISE

Jaxon patted the muscled, black neck of his warhorse. Thrax nickered and lowered his head, demanding a scratch behind the ears, to which Jaxon absently complied. His irritated dragon paced beneath his skin. He should have dismissed Lord Wainright sooner, and because he'd waited too long, the panther lord—Nicula Sorin—owned Amari's contract.

When Kip had told him of Amari's purchase, he'd almost burned the entire platform to the ground, along with his bloody ram master. Only Crispin's quick reflexes saved Rin from a well-deserved scorching. In a rare display of aggression, Crispin had ordered Jaxon to regain control of his beast. Only his nest brother could have spoken to him in such a manner and lived to see another day.

Jaxon shook his head, trying to clear his muddled brain. Herbivores had never interested his dragon, so the sudden infatuation over the little redhead mystified him. Predators of his caliber didn't mix with herbs due to their docile nature. So why had he almost charred the entire field over Amari's contract going to another?

He should be happy for her; Nicula was a powerful and fair lord who could ensure her safety.

Nevertheless, Jaxon's gut churned with his beast stewing in the middle of it.

He tossed the saddle onto Thrax's back with a heavy hand, and his steed grunted. "I'm sorry, my friend," he murmured, regretting his callousness. Jeb Thrax had chosen his animal form after his wife and two young sons were massacred by rogues. Jeb had remained a horse for so long, Jaxon wasn't even sure he could shift back into a man.

He reached for the cinch under Thrax's belly and tightened the strap. Ignoring his surly dragon, he patted Thrax's shoulder. He had never experienced such love for another, and vowed to never put himself in such a vulnerable position by loving someone so completely.

"Sire?"

He turned to find a contrite-looking Rin standing beside Kip, who sat astride his palomino—a true animal, not a shifter.

"The new charges are ready to start homeward at your command," Rin informed him in a subdued tone.

Jaxon's beast pressed against his mind, urging him to strangle Rin for allowing another to purchase their little sheep.

But she isn't ours.

"Good. We'll leave shortly," Jaxon replied, his voice curt.

Rin nodded and scrambled away, leaving Kip, who had an odd expression on his face.

"What?"

Kip shrugged. "Rin didn't know you wanted the redhead."

"What makes you think I did?"

"Your dragon is riding so close to your skin, it almost bit Rin's head off."

Ignoring his youngest cadre brother, Jaxon stepped into the stirrup and swung his leg over Thrax's back. "She's interesting for a throwback; nothing more."

Kip straightened in the saddle. "Suit yourself."

Using pressure and body position, Jaxon encouraged Thrax forward. Kip reined his palomino beside him. "It'll be good to get home."

Jaxon lifted an eyebrow. "I thought you enjoyed the auctions."

Kip nodded. "I do, but..." He hesitated, his blond hair swaying in the breeze.

A protective instinct surged within Jaxon. "What troubles you?" He would deal with anyone who harmed or hurt a member of his cadre...personally.

Crispin's presence filled his mind. *"We're ready to go."*

"Lead us out. Kip and I will bring up the rear."

Crispin acknowledged and closed the link.

A moment later, Jaxon's enhanced hearing registered the groan of leather as horses pulled on straps and wagon wheels creaked with movement.

Thrax pranced and tossed his head, anxious to be underway. With a few strong pats to his mount's neck, Jaxon calmed Thrax and focused on Kip, but didn't press. Although young, Kip was no nestling. War had claimed both of Kip's parents, and even though Jaxon had taken Kip under his wing, the younger man had earned the right to become a member of his cadre and deserved respect.

Kip's yellow-brown eyes latched onto him. "I don't know how you, Crispin, and Slade manage it."

Jaxon's brows furrowed. "Manage what?"

Kip blew out a breath. "Do you know why I come to these auctions?"

Jaxon lifted a shoulder. "To bed women?"

"Not just any woman; my dragon seeks its mate."

"Ahhh."

Even though Kip's beast had grown into a fine and strong animal, both Kip and his dragon were still young. Slade, the third member in his cadre, Crispin, and Jaxon were well into their mature years and should have mated decades ago. Aside from Lord Wainright's daughter, Lorelai, Jaxon knew of no other drakaina. Not that it mattered anyway, since he had chosen his path the day Da left for Mount Kotoa.

"Drakaina are scarce. Our dragons have resigned themselves to the probability we will never find our mate." Jaxon's beast dug its claws into his inner flesh, and he grimaced.

Well, maybe mostly resigned.

Kip sighed. "I know, but my dragon is always searching—in every face and smile, in every woman's walk and laughter. How can you ignore such a desire to be complete?"

Jaxon understood Kip's loneliness, having lived an isolated life for over one hundred eighty years. Since most of the drakaina had died, finding a mate now would be especially difficult. The Seminals—a religious order consisting of aged dragons—preached the goddesses had sent the plague to punish dragon-born for their arrogance. Although Jaxon considered their assertions rubbish, he did fear if breeding pairs continued having trouble conceiving, his kind could someday fall to extinction.

"You mistake resignation with acceptance. Our animals are just as lonely, just as incomplete, but we've matured enough to realize we may never find her." For some reason, his thoughts drifted to Amari and he frowned. *Why would he think about her?*

"I won't settle." Kip's eyes glittered with the ferocity of his conviction.

"We haven't either," Jaxon assured him, although he didn't tell his cadre brother he wasn't looking. Jaxon waggled his eyebrows. "But until we find her, we needn't remain celibate."

Kip's lips twitched, and with the jubilance of youth, his mood changed. "Agreed," he said with a widening grin.

Hooves pounding on the compact soil drew their attention as Crispin galloped his dappled gray down the line of shifters, his body moving in rhythm to the horse's gait, and his black hair flying behind him.

Crispin turned his gray in a wide circle and eased up next to them on Jaxon's right. "We approach Nicula's group. Looks like a wagon lost a wheel and they've pulled off the road to fix it."

Jaxon leaned forward, his dragon already searching. Although he shouldn't encourage his beast by giving Amari additional thought, her fiery personality intrigued him.

"I'll lead the line," Kip volunteered and encouraged his mount into a gallop.

Jaxon barely acknowledged the departure of his cadre brother because the predator inside him had already found her. Nicula's caravan had sought shade off the main road among a cloister of weeping willows. Everyone mingled together in their animal designations, except for Amari, who sat on a boulder away from the others.

"Your sheep sits by herself," Crispin noted. "Not a very sheep thing to do."

Although his dragon didn't deny Crispin's assertion, he did. "She's not *my* sheep."

His sentinel shrugged. "If you say so. I'll stay at the end of the line. Kip and I can handle matters until you catch up." Crispin reined his gray to the right and encouraged his mount into a trot down the row of shifters with a click of his tongue.

Anxious energy swirled inside Jaxon as he nudged Thrax forward.

Was he actually excited to see her?

His dragon seemed to think so.

Amari sat on a large rock with her legs tucked against her chest and her forehead planted on her knees. She hadn't slept well. A part of her brain had refused to shut down with so many strangers inside the tent. She also couldn't get comfortable, and by the early morning hours, alternating chills and hot flashes rumbled through her body. The pain along her left side had increased to the point she could barely tolerate her dress rubbing against her skin.

Her gown proved just as bothersome as her wounded side because it tangled between her legs when she walked fast. How could she defend herself in such clothing? Did sheep even consider such things? With a begrudging sigh, she acknowledged her growing dislike over the sheep status she had given herself. The broken wheel had been an unexpected surprise, and she'd immediately sought a quiet place to wallow in her misery.

"Deep in thought?"

His baritone voice rolled over her and soaked into her skin, fostering the hair on her arms to rise. She inhaled a breath to gather her thoughts and lifted her head. Her eyes widened. A small gasp slipped out before she could catch it, and any further attempt to draw air into her lungs ceased over the larger-than-life male consuming her vision.

Wearing tan pants and a white collared shirt, Lord Jaxon Blackthorn sat astride a magnificent black beast, his elbow resting on the saddle horn. His mount shifted, and Lord Blackthorn's body compensated with an easy grace. The suns at his back cast him in a muted glow, accentuating his cheekbones and rugged jawline. A breeze kicked strands of black hair across his face in a wildness that pleased her. The man before her would never be mistaken for a sheep, and her body hummed in appreciation.

"Resting," she gasped out, wondering when her lungs would start working again.

Lord Blackthorn glanced toward the others. "By yourself?"

"I like being alone," she said with a small shrug. Fidgeting under his stare, she would have squirmed out of her skin and fled into the surrounding forest if possible. Running trembling fingers through her hair, she concentrated on keeping her heart from thumping out of her chest.

He followed her movements, and she sizzled inside. Her head wound must be more severe than she thought because no sane woman would be excited over the hungered focus of this predator.

Jaxon's nostrils flared, and his irises swirled tar pit black, highlighting the amber ring around them. "Are you well?"

If he noticed her discomfort, her appearance had to be more dismal than she suspected. Heat slammed into her cheeks, and she glanced away. "I'm fine. Just tired." Hoping to avoid further discussion about her wayward health, she changed the subject. "You're dragon-born?"

"I am," he answered with a note of pride.

"Then why do you ride a horse instead of fly?"

A mischievous gleam sparkled in his ebony eyes. "Our dragons tend to frighten the herbivores."

"I see." She supposed he was trying to intimidate her, and probably would have been frightened if she could think clearly. But instead, her deranged mind could only deduce that such a beautiful man must make a breathtaking beast.

She had never seen a dragon...at least from what she could remember.

A shudder rippled through her, but not because of her injuries. No, she foolishly trembled like a schoolgirl over the possibility of glimpsing the terrifying animal hiding inside the man.

In a daring display, she latched onto his gaze.

Surprise flickered across his face, then the amber rings encircling his irises thickened, bleeding and blending toward his pupils.

Adrenaline shot through her veins. "Not me. I'd love to see your dragon." Her eyes slipped closed.

How would it feel to soar above the world astride such an intimidating beast...

"...and ride upon its back," she whispered, her voice raspy.

Goddesses! When had the temperature gotten so uncomfortably hot?

She opened her eyes and gaped at the glorious man before her.

Jaxon's beast stared at the little sheep as if she were a tasty treat. Amari may not have realized the effect of her words, but *he* did. Dragons were ferocious—easy to anger, stubborn, and absurdly possessive. Most females, regardless of their designation, shied away from them.

So Amari's desire to ride upon his beast speared Jaxon's heart like an arrow. His thoughts immediately descended to her mounting other parts of his anatomy, and he shifted awkwardly in the saddle. His dragon wholeheartedly agreed and demanded they take her in front of everyone. A small smile tipped his lips. His beast had never been one for social courtesy.

"Will you show me sometime?"

Her voice simmered across his skin in a teasing lilt, pulling him from his lurid thoughts back to the woman on her rocky throne. She looked pale, and from her sunken cheeks, appeared as if she hadn't been eating. A fine sheen of perspiration coated her forehead, although it wasn't warm. An odd sensation squeezed his chest, causing both man and dragon to pause. Worry? Were they concerned over the petite redhead? Once acknowledged, his beast practically jumped out of his skin to protect her.

Yes, totally possessive.

"Will you?" she asked again in a hopeful whisper.

"Will I what?" he asked in return, so lost in his thoughts, he'd forgotten the topic of conversation.

"Let me see your dragon sometime?"

Her inquisitive, emerald eyes peered through her lashes with such a beguiling purity, it fostered a genuine grin from him. He imagined her cheeks would flush a beautiful crimson if she knew her request also happened to be a metaphor for his cock, which strained against his pants. His beast whined, pleading they show her—his dragon, who had never begged for anything during their long life.

"Amari, there you are." Lord Sorin slipped out of the trees, his fluid strides accentuating the agility of the panther inside him. He spotted Jaxon and stopped beside her. "You shouldn't stray too far from the others," Nicula chastised, "because you never know what scoundrels might be lurking about."

Jaxon's dragon snarled. "Good to see you too. Cough up any hairballs lately?"

Nicula opened his mouth wide, showcasing his fangs. "Only a few bits of charred dragon."

The tiny gasp that slipped out of Amari stilled Jaxon's reply. Again, unease crept over him like a shadow. He didn't want to be the one who caused her discomfort.

"It's alright, Lady Amari," Nicula soothed. "The lizard is tame enough."

Her mouth dropped open.

Although Amari's innocence tugged at Jaxon's heart, he couldn't silence his laughter, followed by Nicula's hearty bellow.

Her eyes frosted, and from her clamped jaw, she didn't find their bantering amusing. Although her flaming red cheeks only made her more appealing, she seemed intent on escaping.

"You are right, Lord Sorin. I will endeavor to be more careful," she replied in a clipped tone, then slid off the rocks.

If his dragon hadn't been so focused on her, the slight grimace might have gone unnoticed. Again, he inhaled a deep breath, filtering out Amari's scent from the rest. Although he couldn't be sure, a sickly-sweet aroma entwined with her cinnamon scent.

His dragon whimpered over her departure...so did the man.

Nicula stepped forward and extended his hand, and he grabbed the panther's forearm. "How are you, Nic?"

Thrax turned his head and nickered softly, offering his own greeting.

Nicula scratched behind Thrax's ear. "Hello to you too, old friend. I hope you are well and your pain gone," he said with an affectionate pat before focusing on Jaxon. "Except for the bad crop last year, all is well. We are hoping to recover by expanding our planting acreage. I came to the auction to acquire more help."

Jaxon nodded, but his gaze remained fixed on the gentle sway of a certain redhead's hips until she disappeared within a flock of sheep shifters. Although small for a dragon mate, she moved with a poise that belied strength and determination.

"She is interesting, isn't she?"

The sudden bout of jealousy churning in Jaxon's gut caught him off guard more than Nicula's question. "She's different," he replied with a shrug. "Why did you purchase her contract?"

"I enjoy the oddities in life and have not seen one like her in many seasons. She held her own on the platform in front of the others. I admire her courage." Nicula's gaze shifted toward the group of shifters sequestering their topic of conversation. "Those lords don't even realize what they let go."

Jaxon's dragon wanted to negotiate for her, but Nicula would never part with something he considered unique. And Amari was one of a kind.

"Treat her well," Jaxon said before he could stop himself, and the underlying threat didn't go unnoticed.

Nicula's dark eyes softened. "'Tis a shame she's an herb, is it not, dragon?"

Jaxon smiled. "Safe journey."

"You as well."

With a brush of his heels, Thrax jumped forward at full gallop, chasing after the caravan. Jaxon's beast howled in protest.

There's nothing I can do. We were too late, and she's a sheep for the love of the goddesses. We'd end up killing her. At least with Nicula, she'll be safe.

Although his dragon shifted to a dark corner of his mind to sulk, his beast didn't agree with his argument, and Jaxon wasn't sure if he did either.

CHAPTER 10

FINDERS KEEPERS

Nolan stepped through the swinging doors and entered the dingy bar. His beast snarled over the odor of stale fermented oats, sweat, and unwashed shifters. Unaffected by the dim light, he scanned the shabby establishment.

Four groups of herbivores huddled in booths along the west wall while three predators perched on stools at the bar. He walked past the herbs, his footfalls echoing in the confined space. Sensing the predator within him, the herbivores kept their eyes averted, but his dragon still growled over being in the company of such filth.

Nolan smiled. Years of living with the Eldians had turned his animal into a snob.

By the auctioneer's description, the trader Nolan sought sat on the stool farthest from the door, so he took the empty seat beside him.

The man's right hand stilled on his glass while his left disappeared beneath the counter.

Nolan's dragon leaned forward. Although his beast might consider itself cultured now, it still loved a good fight. "I'm looking for someone." Nolan kept his voice low, but surmised everyone in the bar heard, since all talking had ceased the moment he stepped through the double doors.

"That so?"

His dragon bared its teeth. "Female, short red hair."

"Don't know her." The trader lifted the glass to his lips. "You should have asked the auctioneer."

"I did. How do you think I found you? But the auctioneer scurried down a rabbit hole before I could ask additional questions." Nolan frowned. "I might have been a little overzealous."

The other two predators slid off their stools and spaced themselves at Nolan's back. From their smell, he guessed they were wolves. His beast was practically hopping up and down over the impending fight. "She would be hard to miss with her red hair."

The trader slid his empty glass down the bar for the bartender to refill. Swiveling on his stool to face him, he eyed Nolan with the disdain of a predator almost at the top of the food chain...*almost*. "Said I don't know her. Now bugger off, weasel dick."

Weasel dick? Did Nolan's beast just hear that right? This predator had a death wish because anyone who threatened the size of Nolan's cock, had no intention of remaining above ground for long. In a blur of motion, Nolan grabbed the trader's wrist, then reached for the knife at the man's belt. With a *ting* and a *thunk*, the blade sliced through the wolf's hand and embedded into the bar top.

The trader howled. "You're a dead man," he snarled past his elongating incisors.

Nolan sensed the increased heat signatures from the predators behind him as they too began to shift. The fools were so intent on killing him, they didn't even notice the man standing at the entrance, his shadow spilling across the wood-stained floor.

"Nolan," drawled the man at the door.

"Bastaine," he acknowledged.

"Did you have to draw blood? My dragon is starving."

Nolan shrugged. "This guy has a memory problem. I'm helping him remember."

Bastaine stepped into the room. As soon as he cleared the threshold, the herbs in the booths abandoned their drinks and fled the tavern.

"I don't want trouble," the bartender announced while reaching under the counter.

Bastaine raised his hand. "We'll pay for any damages."

The bartender relaxed. "Just make sure I have a building left to fix, dragon."

Bastaine nodded. "Fair 'nough."

Satisfied, the bartender stepped away from the counter to clean up the vacated tables.

Bastaine dropped onto the stool beside Nolan, and rested his back against the bar top so he could monitor the two other predators, who no longer showed signs of shifting.

Nolan smiled. Although young, Bastaine stood over six-three. His well-proportioned, muscled body caused many a woman to swoon, and most men to think twice. Although Bastaine had already attained the age of maturity, he still acted with the brash arrogance of a young dragon who was still finding himself. The vibrant ocher ring encircling Bastaine's light hazel eyes pulsed with a bright glow.

The shifters at Nolan's back shuffled on their feet. "Dorn, we'll wait for you outside," muttered the wiser of the two.

"Good idea," Bastaine said and flashed his famous smile that won the hearts of the toughest females.

Nolan shook his head, still gripping the hilt of the blade embedded in Dorn's hand. "You always knew how to clear a room," he told his younger nest brother.

"Occupational hazard. Now get on with it, so we can get out of this pit."

The bartender growled.

"But it's a nice pit," Bastaine added with a sheepish grin.

Nolan looked at the wolf. "Where was I?"

Sweat coated Dorn's forehead. "You're a dragon?"

Bastaine snorted. "Dumbass."

Nolan's remaining patience had exited the bar with the herbs. Life was about to get very uncomfortable for the wolf if he didn't start talking. "The redhead, where is she?"

Bastaine growled, his beast riding close to the surface. All dragon males protected the young in their nest, but Amari held a special place within the cadre. As the firstborn female to their alpha, they had watched over her to the point of hovering, and considered her disappearance a personal affront.

"Sold to the panther lord, Nicula Sorin," the shifter ground out.

Nolan's beast snarled. "You sold her into servitude?"

"Of course," Dorn panted. "Along with the other sheep."

"She wasn't meant for servitude."

"I bought her fair and square." The arteries in Dorn's neck bulged from his clenched teeth. "And I didn't even want her because she was hurt, but the tracker said it was an all or nothing deal."

Panic soured Nolan's stomach. "How bad were her injuries?"

"I don't know," Dorn whined. His good hand gripped the bar in a white-knuckled hold.

Nolan twisted the knife, and Dorn screamed.

"Not bad, I swear. Some other dragons also were interested in her before the panther bought her contract."

Nolan glanced at Bastaine whose eyes gleamed. Bastaine's beast appeared close to reducing the entire place to ash. The barkeep had been right to worry.

"Who are these other dragons?"

Blood pooled around the shifter's hand. His entire body shook, and from his ashen skin color, he seemed about to pass out. "Lord Blackthorn and his cadre."

"His cadre?" Nolan blew out a stunned breath. "Yet she went to the panther?"

Dorn nodded. "Please, let me go."

"Where does Sorin live?"

"Somewhere in the Junipine Wetlands." Dorn's voice cracked. "I know nothing more, I swear."

Nolan pulled the knife from the shifter's hand before the wolf could muster another scream. With two quick swipes, he cleaned the bloody blade on the back of Dorn's shirt and stood.

Bastaine threw some coins on the bar, and they were out the door and into the bright sunlight without a backward glance.

"Why do you think the dragons were interested in her?" Bastaine asked.

Nolan shrugged. "Not sure."

"She could be experiencing the awakening."

Both men released their dragons and jumped skyward, rising with the effortless sweep of their large wings.

"Her mother is Eldian," Nolan insisted.

"What does that matter?" Bastaine countered. *"If she is in the first stages, then she won't know how to control the urges developing within her. We must find her before Trinity."*

"We will." Fear curled around Nolan's heart like an asp about to strike. He had watched over Amari since birth—a small squall of a baby, with pink cheeks and chubby arms and legs. He'd be damned if he let any harm befall her now.

CHAPTER 11

ATTACKED

To make up time, Sorin's caravan traveled most of the day, stopping only to eat a quick lunch. The flat, grassy plains eventually gave way to rocky terrain, forcing Amari to watch her footing to avoid twisting an ankle. Although she started out strong, her pace slowed as morning drifted into afternoon, and by the time the suns dipped low on the horizon, her position had slipped to the last straggler. Most of the shifters were already resting or washing in a nearby stream by the time she stumbled into camp.

Using a tree trunk as a backrest, she snoozed for a while until the clatter of the chow bell woke her, but she couldn't muster any enthusiasm for another plate of greens. Her side had morphed into a massive hot spot. Chills coursed through her body, but if the pattern held, she would soon be drenched in sweat.

She shook her head to clear her vision, and considered seeking the healer before dozing off to the delicious aroma of cooking meat from the predator tents.

She awoke after the camp had settled down for the night. One moon monitored the land in an eerie blue-white hue while the top of the second poked above the edge of the world.

To alleviate the tedium of walking all day, she had eavesdropped on conversations, hoping any tidbit of information would act as a catalyst for her memory. Many of the young shifters had talked about the approaching Trinity moon and transition week. From what she could gather, the small moon appeared during the fall solstice and joined the regular two moons. For seven days, adult two-souls shifted into their animal to charge their bodies under the combined energies of the three moons.

First transitions always occurred during Trinity, marking the passage from youth to adulthood. While it sounded like a time of celebration, evidently it could also be dangerous for those who failed to shift into their animal.

The higher moon disappeared behind a thin line of clouds, thickening the gloom around her. She stared at the pale orb, bathing the land in a muted light. Wind whispered in the treetops above, lulling her in a rare moment of contentment as she let the soft noises of the night seduce her even though her parched throat demanded attention.

She probed her split bottom lip with her tongue, then struggled to her feet. Using the tree for support, she waited for her pulse to slow and the land to stop spinning before plodding toward the sweet rumble of water. After alleviating her thirst, she would find the healer.

Using the rising moons' glow, she walked across the uneven landscape until she reached the river. The water glittered in a silvery shimmer of undulating movement, pushing its way to an unknown destination.

She spread her arms to balance herself and shuffle-stepped down the embankment. With each footfall, she dislodged shale and dirt, sending pebbles tumbling ahead of her. Her momentum instigated a mini avalanche, and her measured steps turned into haphazard leaps until her toe snagged on an exposed root and she tumbled headfirst onto the rocky ground.

Her head exploded in pain, but that didn't compare to the agony searing her side. Forcing slow, even breaths through her nose, she clamped her jaw to silence the scream and curled into a ball, praying for the hurt to end.

She lay on the damp soil long after the second moon had reached its zenith and began chasing after the first in its downward journey. The roar of the water drowned out all sound. She closed her eyes and lost herself to the raging river, but the chilly ground kept her from falling asleep. After another bout of time, she rolled onto her hands and knees and crawled to the water. Resting on her knees, she cupped the water to her mouth. The first moon had dipped below the horizon, and soon the smaller moon would succumb, leaving dawn and the twin suns to watch over the land.

With her thirst sated, she would now find the healer. Pushing to her feet, she eyed the steep embankment. Knowing she couldn't retrace her steps, she headed downstream until an animal trail gleamed in the pale light.

The path wove through the woods. Old oaks towered above her. Although walking unaccompanied in an unknown forest should terrify her, she welcomed the serenity until the sounds of screams and clashing swords shattered the silence. Her heart kicked. Even though she could have stayed hidden within her sanctuary, something inside her encouraged her forward. At the forest edge, she hid behind a tree and peered around the trunk.

Chaos engulfed the camp. Rogues streamed from the trees opposite the clearing like a wildebeest stampede—slicing, hacking, and stabbing their way through the helpless herbivore shifters.

Panthers, leopards, wolves, lions, and an assortment of smaller cats formed a line to meet the onslaught. Having transformed into their animals, Nicula's men counterattacked with a savagery of their own, defending the herbs under their care. Their fangs and claws glistened like daggers in the moonlight. Although they fought with an unforgiving viciousness equal to the rogues, they were outnumbered.

A panther with vivid green eyes raced past her and leapt onto the back of a rogue who had just beheaded a woman. The rogue pitched back and forth, lurching across the field in a macabre-like dance with the cat hanging on until the rogue's energy waned. In a final show of strength, the cat buried its fangs into the rogue's throat and ripped it open, then disappeared into the fray before the rogue's body hit the ground.

Flames shot skyward from burning tents and wagons, illuminating the darkness in blurred images of horror. Missing limbs, eviscerated bodies, and the charred remains of herbs littered the trampled earth amid pools of blood.

She should help, but what could she do without a weapon? Fear and indecision coalesced into anger. Mindless creatures were slaughtering innocent people. She stepped away from the sheltering trees.

Her actions were foolish at best, deadly at worst. She should be running from the battle, not walking toward it.

Panthers and leopards raced past her while herbs scrambled in every direction like roaches fleeing a sinking ship. Adrenaline flooded her body, pushing blood into her muscles and heightening her senses, but a low groan brought her up short.

Still holding his dagger, a fallen shifter clutched his belly. Although his hands kept his intestines inside his belly, he couldn't stem the dark red flow streaming through his fingers.

Tears blurred her vision. She might not be a healer, but even she knew he would soon leave this world. She recognized this man—a panther shifter, and part of Nicula's pack. Dropping to her knees, she brushed matted, black hair off his face.

His eyes snapped open. "Go," he commanded through gritted teeth. "Find the trees...where it's safe."

She glanced at the pandemonium around her, then focused her attention on him. "I'll stay."

"Go!" His one-word decree zapped his last bit of strength and his head lolled to the side.

Amari squared her shoulders. "I'm sorry, but I don't think I've ever been one to do as I'm told."

Although glazed with pain, his eyes remained clear. An amused smile crossed his lips before twisting into a grimace. "What is y—"

Liquid coughs from lungs filling with blood swallowed his words as she stroked his face. Maybe his impending death, or her need to confide, infused her with courage. Whatever the reason, the words spilled out of her in a long rush of air. "I don't know my designation. I don't remember."

His simple nod of acceptance overwhelmed her. She longed to belong somewhere…anywhere.

He held up his dagger. "Take it."

She wrapped her hand around his, keeping the blade within his grip. Concentrating only on his face to avoid the horror of his ravaged body, she skimmed her fingers across his cheek. She wanted to remain strong for him, but her silly heart got in the way and tears bubbled over her lashes.

"Tell my brother to look after Trey."

"I will."

His body relaxed, and he stopped breathing. She whispered a silent prayer for his safe passage to the Everlasting, then unwrapped his fingers from the dagger to palm the bloody hilt. "I will not let your death be for nothing."

A twig snapped behind her. Her heart thumped once, then surged into a wild rhythm. Keeping her movements casual, she released the panther's hand and bowed her head, as if in mourning, but strained to hear a clue that would help her reveal what stalked her. Her hands shook.

Should she run or fight?

She was small and didn't stand a chance.

Or did she?

Testing the dagger's weight, the weapon nestled against her palm like an old friend. She angled her head and listened, muffled grunts and chuffing breaths her only warning. Resting the blade along her forearm, she twisted and rose, slashing upward.

A semi-shifted man, with tusks and the coarse hair of a boar, dropped his short sword and clutched his throat to stem the blood streaming through his fingers from a severed carotid. He fell to his knees and toppled over before growing still.

His blood dotted her arms and the rest of her body, but she paid no attention to it. She knew how to use a blade? *Why* did she know how to use a weapon? *Who* had taught her?

She surveyed the carnage around her. Emptiness threatened to gobble her up whole. Who in the seven hells was she? She bit her tongue to keep from shouting her frustration to the heavens.

Tremors rocked her body. She had just killed a man, yet felt no regret. Bending over, she inhaled deep breaths to ease the urge to empty her stomach. Instead of fearing for the salvation of her soul, something inside her clicked into place. She was strong, had always been strong, and would kill without remorse to protect herself.

A shriek startled her from her thoughts, and she looked around. Smoke engulfed the clearing, searing her eyes, but she could just make out the form of a young child.

"Camden!" she screamed and rushed toward him as he stumbled out of the haze.

"I can't find my mom," he sobbed, tears streaking down his dirt-smudged cheeks.

She dropped to one knee in front of him. "We'll find her," she promised. "But first, let's get you safe."

His tiny arms encircled her waist as if fearing she would leave him.

"Can you run, Camden?"

Large, innocent brown eyes stared back at her. "Mom says I'm really fast."

"Good." She smiled. "See the trees behind me? We're going to race to them."

He looked past her toward the woods, and his face twisted in panic. She reached out to reassure him until she realized something behind her had frozen the small child in terror. Fear of being too late slid down her spine, but she cradled the blade along her inner arm, and once again, spun and slashed outward in a flowing movement that could only have been perfected from years of practice. Blood splayed in all directions as another rogue fell from her newly acquired dagger.

Without further delay, she grabbed Camden's hand. His little legs pumped hard, struggling to keep up with her pace. They reached the forest edge, barreled into the shadows beneath the towering evergreens, and continued running until Camden fell to his knees.

Not satisfied they were far enough away, she picked him up. Her side erupted in pain, but she ignored it and pushed deeper into the woods. Only when her legs could no longer support them, did she crawl beneath a shrub and drag Camden in beside her. The boy huddled against her. Gripping the dagger in one hand, she curled her free arm around him and patted his back. To drown out the distant shouts and screams, she hummed a song she didn't remember the words to until the cries of battle faded and Camden's ragged breathing eased into deep, even breaths.

Staring into the darkness, she listened to the night sounds of the great forest. Crickets chirped and small creatures scurried past, yet instead of alarm, she relaxed. The bed of leaves cushioned her body while the trees enveloped her in a sense of belonging. For the moment, they were safe. The woods would watch over them.

Amari closed her eyes and succumbed to her exhaustion.

CHAPTER 12

REMAINS

"Find her, Crispin," Jaxon ordered.

Crispin nodded and jumped off his gray. With two running steps, he shifted, and his powerful wings propelled him into the soot-filled sky.

Jaxon dismounted Thrax and walked toward Nicula and another panther shifter, both of whom were crouched over a body. He scanned the devastation as he approached them. The smell of blood and death seared his nostrils. Wagons smoldered like beacons, warning others away. The soft cries of those mourning loved ones filled his ears. Only two tents had survived the madness and had been turned into aid stations. Both were filled to capacity while a single harried healer scurried about, shouting orders.

He opened his mental link with Dax, the commander of his guard, and told him to bring the healer they had just acquired at the auction to assist with the wounded. His dragon pressed close, and Jaxon clenched his teeth, sharing his beast's sentiments. They didn't like arriving late to the party. With an indifferent glance at a dead boar rogue, he sidestepped the thickened pool of blood and stood a discreet distance from the grieving men.

Nicula looked up, his hand clasping the dark-haired man's shoulder, who knelt beside the shifter's body.

"The smoke drew us here. I'm sorry we didn't arrive sooner."

Nicula nodded, but his attention returned to the young man, whom Jaxon recognized.

Gavin, a panther shifter, was holding his dead brother's hand. A blood-stained bandage covered his bicep, but Gavin seemed oblivious to his physical pain. Some cat shifter families bonded in tight packs and experienced loss on a deep level.

"I'm sorry about your brother," Jaxon said, offering the young panther his condolences.

With a shuddered breath, Gavin stood. "I'll scout for survivors," he said, his voice thick.

Nicula appeared as if he was about to argue, but instead, his gaze softened. "Very well. I'll have Emun attend to your brother."

Gavin tipped his head to acknowledge Jaxon before walking away.

Nicula ran a hand through his black hair. "Gabe was a good man. He'll be missed."

Jaxon's dragon paced beneath his skin, anxious to find Amari. "What happened here?"

"Soon after we parted yesterday, scouts spotted someone following us."

"Any idea who?"

"No. They evaded my men." Nicula's lips pressed in a firm line. "And I sent pack members to search for them."

Jaxon understood Nicula's meaning. Nic's pack had an unparalleled reputation for tracking and capturing their quarry. They were not used to failure.

"We pushed the caravan hard, choosing the middle of the clearing as our campsite so we would see them coming if they left the trees."

"Who attacked you?"

Nicula's hands curled into fists. "Rogues."

Jaxon's eyebrows lifted. "A few rogues couldn't have done this much damage."

"They were packing. Over fifty streamed from the forest."

Jaxon shook his head. "Rogues don't run in groups."

Nicula's black eyes hardened. "These did, and they were organized."

Jaxon's thoughts drifted to Amari. Apprehension turned his stomach sour. *Crispin should have found her by now.*

"They were driving herbs into the woods. We managed to keep most together and protected, but some bolted. And look here." Nicula toed the ground beside the dead boar.

Jaxon noticed the object next to the rogue's hand. "A net?"

Nicula nodded. "Many of the rogues were carrying nets."

"To capture herbs?"

"I assume so." Nicula shrugged, his dark eyes unreadable.

"I've never heard of rogues taking prisoners. Have you?"

Nicula glanced around the clearing, his expression grim. "No, but I've never seen them pack like this either."

Jaxon's dragon snarled, the smell of blood agitating his beast. Tension kept his body taut. "The redhead?"

Nicula placed a hand on Jaxon's shoulder. "I don't know."

"Jax." Crispin's voice filled his head. *"She's not in the meadow."*

"Expand your search. Nicula said the rogues tried to scatter the herbs. Maybe she escaped into the woods."

"Very well."

"Nic!" Gavin yelled, waving them over to where he crouched beside a mottled patch of churned up soil. "See here…" Gavin pointed, "…and here? One set of tracks leading away from my brother before meeting up with another set. Both tracks head for the woods."

Jaxon studied the tracks. "Rogues?"

Gavin hesitated. "The impressions aren't deep enough for a man. My guess is a female and a child."

"Can you follow them?" Nicula asked.

"Yes."

"I'll go with him." Jaxon's willingness to protect Gavin's back so the panther could focus on the trail was based on more than simple alliances. His reasons were also selfish. The smell of battle called to the wild nature of his beast, and coupled with the unknown whereabouts of Amari, he could barely keep his dragon contained.

"Thank you. I appreciate your help." Nicula nodded at Gavin. "Off you go."

Gavin pivoted and sprinted toward the woods. In a sizzle of light, he shifted into his panther, with Jaxon running close behind.

CHAPTER 13

A GUILTY MIND

izbet's footfalls echoed off the marble walls as she padded down the passage toward her parent's chambers. Her blue silk gown swished with the sway of her hips.

While most Eldians preferred living near wooded forests, her father had built a fortress directly inside a mountain. Even though she never understood why they lived differently, she had grown up loving the rugged majesty of their home. With expansive rooms, wide hallways and open-air balconies, she always felt at peace within these walls. Although Father boasted their fortress was a mighty stronghold, she just considered the place home.

Lizbet stopped at the elaborate doors to her parent's suite. A male dragon, breathing fire and standing protectively over a drakaina, greeted her. With painstaking care, an Eldian craftsman had etched the dragons into the thick oak doors. She traced her fingers across the male's wing. Even after all these years, the beauty of the regal creatures still amazed her. If only she had someone who cherished her as much as the male sheltering the female in the carving.

Closing her mind to such thoughts, she stiffened her spine and rapped on the door. Mother's muffled voice filtered through the thick wood, and she pushed the doors open and stepped into the spacious room. To the left, a quilt to an impressive canopy bed lay unruffled, and an inviting fire flickered in the stone fireplace, but no one enjoyed its warmth. Scanning to her right, she spotted Mother out on the grand balcony, sitting on a bench swing.

Leaden feet propelled her across the floor, laden with rugs woven by the finest Eldian artisans, until she stopped beside Selena, who smiled up at her.

"Sit, dear one." Mother patted the cushion next to her.

Without hesitation, Lizbet complied. She always did what she was told, and therein was the problem. Maybe Amari wouldn't be missing if she'd challenged Amari's mandate to return home and get help. In her twenty-first season, she would be an adult soon and needed to behave like one by trusting her instincts.

Mother's arm skirted around her and pulled her close. "Talk to me."

Lizbet's guilt almost choked the words from her mouth. "I shouldn't have left her. Amari's lost because of me."

Once spoken, the reality of her sister's disappearance hit home and the floodgates opened. Tears washed down her cheeks and darkened her dress wherever the drops splashed.

"Shhh," Selena cooed, wrapping both arms around her.

Mother's comfort intensified her guilt. She buried her head into the folds of Selena's gown and wept for the ache in her heart, for her lack of courage, and for the anguish she'd caused her parents. But most of all, she cried for obeying Amari, when she should have stayed and helped. Losing sense of time, she let Mother rock them back and forth long after the tears had stopped.

"Your father and his cadre will find her," Selena assured. "If you had remained, they would have captured you too. I wouldn't have survived losing both of you. Have faith in Greyson and his men. They won't rest until Amari is found."

Lizbet pushed out of Mother's arms. "Do you really believe so?"

Selena's genuine smile lightened the darkness in her heart. "Without a doubt, and I can only imagine the stories Amari will have to tell."

Despite herself, a small smile crossed Lizbet's lips—Amari always found trouble.

The chamber doors slamming shut drew her attention an instant before Father's voice boomed across the foyer. "How fare my lovely ladies?"

She jumped up and bolted into Greyson's arms. "Have you found her?"

"Not yet, my dove, but Nolan and Bastaine have a good lead. I expect her home soon. Now, you don't want to be late, so scoot."

She bit her bottom lip. "It doesn't feel right taking an archery lesson without Amari."

Greyson rested his large hand over his heart, feigning distress. "Please, go as a favor to me. Otherwise your grandda will get grouchy and your mother will force me to dine with him."

"Greyson!" Selena admonished with a shake of her head.

Lizbet searched her father's face. "Are you sure they'll find her?"

"Positive," Greyson answered, noting the anguish in his daughter's copper eyes. He would gladly shoulder his girls' pain to ensure their happiness, including the one carrying his unborn child. "Go my sweet dove, and don't fret. We'll have your sister home soon."

"Yes, Father." Lizbet grabbed his collar and pulled him down for a quick kiss on the cheek before scampering for the door.

Once alone, he sat beside his mate. In a shift of dominance, Selena leaned into his chest and he wrapped an arm around her. Drawing her legs beneath her, he assumed the task of swinging them.

"Any news?" she asked.

He kissed the top of Selena's head. Although not a shifter, his mate was no pampered royal either. She had always possessed a lion's courage, but now with two girls filling their nest, and another child on the way, even he would think twice about challenging her.

"Nolan and Bastaine found the trader who sold her into servitude. She went to a panther near the wetlands."

Selena's delicate hand settled on his chest. His dragon purred as her fingers splayed wide in a possessive claim. "But she isn't bound by the laws of servitude. Why doesn't she just come home?"

Greyson frowned. He had wondered the same thing. Although his eldest had an adventurous spirit, she wouldn't be so reckless to cause her family such distress. "She's not acting herself," he admitted.

"Do you think it's the awakening?" Selena lifted her head, her eyes filled with concern.

His dragon whined, longing to ease her distress. He buried his fingers through the folds of Selena's auburn hair before encouraging her head to his shoulder. Although an alpha female, he had long ago established his right to be her mate. "Don't worry about Trinity. We'll have her back before then."

"Do you think she's scared? Maybe we should have told her what lives within her?"

He stroked the back of Selena's neck with his thumb. Out of his two girls, Amari's wild disposition catered to the arrogant nature of her beast. Under normal circumstances, he would have welcomed the coming solstice and appearance of Amari's drakaina for the first time. But since Amari was half-Eldian, and one-souls didn't carry an animal or experience the effects of Trinity, they had deemed Amari's transition too dangerous and had taken precautions years ago to ensure she never experienced it.

He squeezed his mate's shoulder and rested his chin atop her head. "When we almost lost her as a baby, we decided not to subject her to Trinity. I'll not have you second-guess our decision now."

Selena swung her legs so they draped across his lap, and his hand found her thigh. He inhaled his mate's evergreen scent—his heartbeat, his life.

His body stirred. The casual swirl of her fingers stroking his chest exacerbated the desire building in his groin.

"But to deny her drakaina life, do we have such a right?"

He enfolded Selena within his arms. By preventing Amari from transitioning this year, they would forever deny her the ability to shift and experience the grace and power of her beast. Even though it pained him to deny Amari the opportunity of knowing her animal, he couldn't bear losing his daughter. He had lost too much in his life and protected what was his to cherish. Both he and his dragon ensured it.

"As her parents, we are duty bound to keep our nestlings safe from harm." His hand skimmed up Selena's arm and cupped her chin. With gentle pressure, he tilted her head and brushed his lips across hers—a soft, measured taste. She opened for him, and he kissed her with a hunger that left them breathless.

She pulled away, and he chuckled at the crimson flare in her cheeks. After all these years, his mate still took his breath away. His hand settled on her still-flat belly. "How is our youngest?"

She entwined her fingers through his. "Safe and loved, knowing she's not alone." Selena's voice broke.

He lifted Selena's chin with his thumb. Her emerald eyes shimmered with tears, the unshed droplets like darts to his heart. He missed Amari with a fierceness that threatened to overwhelm him, so he could only imagine Selena's pain at the loss of their firstborn.

He rested his forehead against hers and cradled her oval face between his callused hands. For a moment, he shut out the world and focused on his stunning mate. "We'll find her, love, and bring her back."

She nodded, dislodging two droplets. They slipped down her cheeks and trailed over his hands. "I believe you, mate of mine," she said with a quaver in her voice.

Unable to withstand her distress, he kissed her. A tender claiming, meant to comfort, but when she pressed against him and dug her hands into his hair, his dragon roared.

His arms tightened around her in a possessive understanding that she would never escape him. If she fell, he would catch her. If she stumbled, he'd right her, and if she ever lost her way, he would find her. So when his mate, the keeper of his heart, murmured against his mouth that she needed to forget, he didn't hesitate and unfurled his body from the swing.

She wrapped her toned legs around his waist, and he carried her to the bed, their tongues tangling in a heated dance. With the gentle attentiveness of a dragon enraptured by its mate, he laid her down and followed her. She fit perfectly beneath him, confirming the goddesses had created her just for him—a gift he would treasure for the rest of his life and beyond.

CHAPTER 14

FOUND

lthough Jaxon could track, his skill didn't match Gavin's panther. They pushed deeper into the woods. The dense trees unsettled Jaxon's dragon, who wanted to break free from the confining space. Ignoring his beast's unease, he stuck close to the panther shifter. After backtracking and reestablishing their trail only once, Gavin sat on his haunches as a man, his fingers tracing the edge of a boot print.

Tree trunks, wider than the span of Jaxon's arms, and thick shrubs surrounded him, caging his beast. He inhaled the ancient forest, dank and rich from age. They had traveled into the heart of the woods. Crispin's voice filled his mind.

"I'm approaching on your left," Crispin warned just as he stepped from behind a large evergreen.

Jaxon eyed his sentinel. *"Any sign of her?"*

Crispin shook his head.

"You think she's dead?"

Crispin shrugged a broad, leather clad shoulder. *"I don't know, but we're deep in the forest. I can't imagine a sheep shifter venturing this far from the flock."*

Crispin's words spurred an unfamiliar disquiet. A strange tightness squeezed Jaxon's chest and spread outward. His dragon whined, as thoughts bombarded his mind. He fought to push them aside, but they persisted. He should have been at her side last night, protecting her.

Gavin stepped toward a bush with thick limbs and dark green leaves. Raising a hand to ensure silence, he crouched and peered into the foliage.

Following the panther's lead, Jaxon knelt and peered into the shadowed undergrowth. Two terror-filled eyes stared back at him. "Come here, boy."

With an almost imperceptible shake of his head, the boy burrowed deeper against the body beside him. Jaxon's gaze sharpened on the slim figure lying amidst the leaves. Before he even spied her telltale hair color, his dragon's shuddered relief echoed through him. He edged forward, ignoring Gavin's curious expression.

"Amari," he whispered. Her name rolled off his tongue like he'd been calling after her for a lifetime.

She whimpered and her dazzling eyes drifted open. "Jaxon?"

Her murmured response rifled straight to his heart—the most beautiful word she could have spoken.

Amari *hurt.* Exhaustion enveloped her in a fog. The earth cushioned her body and the ancient oaks protected her, but even from her cocooned sanctuary, his voice permeated the depths of her weary brain. Although she longed to fall back to sleep, she couldn't deny his call and kept her eyes open even though a mean sprite had replaced her eyelids with sandpaper. Fire licked down her throat. What she wouldn't give for a sip of water.

Unease pooled in her belly, and her heart flip-flopped. Panic choked the breath from her lungs.

Where in the bloody blazes was *she?*

"Amari." He spoke her name again in a low, guttural tone that whispered along her skin and eased her distress. Lord Blackthorn would protect her until she remembered. She glanced up and fell headfirst into two pools of black fire. Her heart settled into a natural rhythm. Yes, Jaxon would watch over her until she figured things out.

"What happened?" her voice rasped over parched vocal cords.

"The caravan was attacked," he reminded softly and reached for her. "Come out of there."

She recoiled. Why would she want to leave the safety of her little nest?

Camden lifted his head off her shoulder. His bottom lip trembled. "Do you think they found my mom?" he whispered in her ear.

Camden's question seared a path through her muddled mind, and the events of last night slammed into her frontal lobe like a sledgehammer. Her arm tightened around Camden's small body. "Let's go see."

Camden nodded. "I miss my ma."

She kissed the boy's forehead. If one so young could be so brave, then she could too.

"Amari, take my hand." Lord Blackthorn wriggled his fingers.

She squeezed Camden's shoulder. "Follow me out."

The boy nodded, his eyes saucer-wide.

A fierce protectiveness swept over her. "No one will hurt you, Camden. I swear it."

The boy smiled. "I know."

Amari slipped her hand into Lord Blackthorn's and warmth shot down her arm. He helped her out, and her mind swam over her sudden vertical position. She swayed, but Jaxon pulled her close to keep her from falling. Under different circumstances, she might have relished his body against hers, but his touch rousted a hornet's nest of pain. Gasping, she stepped away and almost fell again before righting herself.

Lord Blackthorn pursued her. "Are you hurt?" He grabbed her arm, offering support.

A strange tingling sensation spread outward from his hand. His concern encouraged her to seek shelter in his arms, but until she remembered her past, she could trust no one. Choking down her discomfort, she straightened her shoulders. "I'm fine."

From his clenched jaw, he didn't seem convinced.

Sucking in a breath, she bent and helped Camden out of the thicket. The boy scurried around her and watched the three men from behind her back. She widened her stance and waited for the ground to stop spinning.

"You carry a nice blade."

She recognized the man with the small silver earring, and black hair slicked back in a queue as one of Nicula's pack—a panther.

She raised the dagger. "It was given to me."

"My twin never would have parted with the blade our father designed specifically for us." Gavin stepped toward her, his tawny eyes glittering. "I forgive you for taking it, but you will return it now," he said, extending his hand.

She supposed she should have given him the dagger, especially since he had just lost his sibling, and the weapon held sentimental value. But his brother had given it to her, and relinquishing it seemed like a betrayal of her promise to honor his sacrifice.

Although she spoke her refusal with a calm assurance that startled her, her grip tightening on the dagger baffled her even more because a part of her actually wanted him to try to take it.

Gavin stepped toward her.

She bladed her stance and palmed the knife. Anxious energy swirled inside her, but Blackthorn's challenging snarl stopped the panther's approach.

Camden yelped and tucked his head against the small of her back.

Confusion clouded her mind. Why would she want to confront the panther?

"That dagger belongs in my family, Blackthorn."

"Now is not the time," Jaxon shot back.

Gavin whirled on the dragon lord. "I won't have someone who stole it off my dead brother disgrace him by keeping it."

Jaxon's eyes pulsed with an amber glow, as one of his hands curled into a fist and the other reached for his sword.

"Enough," Amari commanded. "Your brother gave it to me before he died. He told me to tell you to take care of Trey."

Gavin's face contorted in sorrow, and she regretted her blunt delivery. "I'm sorry. Since I'm not a healer, I could only hold his hand."

Gavin grimaced.

Tears welled in her eyes. "But I'm grateful for his gift because his dagger saved my life when the boar attacked."

Lord Blackthorn stared at her. "You killed the rogue boar?"

"And another," Camden squeaked. "You really shouldn't make her mad," the boy reprimanded from behind her back.

The men's wide-eyed expressions irritated her. She might be a girl with no past, but in her heart, she'd never been one to back down from a fight. "I won't tolerate any more bickering in front of this boy."

If she wasn't so uncomfortable, she might have been amused over the three men shuffling back and forth on their feet. Giving them her back, she turned to Camden and extended her hand. "Come, little man. Let's go find your mother."

"Yes, ma'am," Camden whispered in an awed voice.

Without a backward glance, she walked away with Camden at her side.

CHAPTER 15

CHOICES MADE

B y the time Amari broke through the trees and slogged into the decimated camp, the bodies had been moved a discreet distance from the tents, and people were halfway through building a pyre. A cloudless sky offered no shelter from the suns' rays, which didn't bode well for the corpses. Although smoke fires acted as a deterrent, soon not even the haze would keep the scavengers away. She glanced at the trees, standing as sentinels on the fringe of the meadow. Buzzards watched from the branches, waiting for their opportunity.

Camden pulled on her hand, tears rimming his eyes. "I don't see her."

The sadness in his voice broke Amari's heart, and she pulled him into a hug. "We'll find her. Don't worry."

Amari stepped toward a tent in search of help when a woman's wail brought her to an abrupt halt. Her grip tightened on the dagger, but the boy yanked free and sped off. "Cam—" Her yell died in her throat as the little ram barreled into his mother's waiting embrace.

Camden's mom peppered him with kisses and hugged him close.

Although happy to see them reunited, a hollow ache thumped in rhythm with Amari's heart. She didn't know such love, or remember it anyway. Did anyone miss her? Was someone desperate to find her?

Camden's mom lifted her head and nodded her thanks before disappearing behind a tent with Camden clutched tightly in her arms.

With a trembling smile for Camden's happy reunion, Amari took a deep breath and entered the first tent. Wounded shifters filled the confined space while two healers rushed about, administering tonics and bandaging wounds. The smell of herbs, antiseptic, and blood wafted to her nostrils.

One of the healers turned, and Amari's eyes widened as the familiar sheep shifter scuttled her way. She had forgotten Lord Blackthorn had purchased Sousa's contract.

"Thank the goddesses, you're alive!" Sousa exclaimed, pulling her into a hug. Amari winced and stepped away.

Sousa's eyes narrowed. "Are you well?"

Her throat constricted, and she shook her head.

"Here." Sousa guided her to an empty mat. "Lie down."

Once settled on the bedding, Sousa closed her eyes and placed her hands on Amari's head. Tendrils of warmth speared inward from Sousa's touch and traveled through her body. For the first time in days, the ache in her temple subsided to a dull throb, then disappeared.

Sousa's hands glided down Amari's body, but Sousa gasped when she reached Amari's side. "Oh, dear," she mumbled.

The soothing flows of healing energy transformed into painful pricks. Amari clenched her teeth to keep from crying out.

With a resigned sigh, Sousa withdrew her hands and opened her eyes. "Why didn't you find a healer sooner?"

The aged woman's voice lashed across Amari's skin like a bullwhip. "I didn't want to bother anyone."

The wrinkles around Sousa's eyes softened, and she brushed the back of her hand down Amari's cheek. "I don't have the power to heal you. Your wounds have grown beyond my ability."

"Will I get better?" Amari hated the tremor in her voice.

Sousa shook her head. "Your injuries are too severe. I can't stop the bleeding."

"How long do I have?"

The healer sighed. "I don't know, but I can ease your pain and make you comfortable."

Since Amari's uncooperative throat had seized again, she could only nod.

Sousa's hand dropped to her shoulder. "Rest now, I'll check on you later."

Curling onto her good side, she watched Sousa shuffle off.

People around her spoke in quiet whispers and kept their eyes averted. Was this how she would spend her last days? A pitied glance here, a hushed murmur there? Amari didn't want the walls of a makeshift tent to be her last memory. She wanted the wind in her face and the sunrise warming her skin. She wanted to *live* her final days, not simply await death.

Two young girls now sat in Sousa's lap, enthralled over her retelling of the creation. The wee ones' giggles began to attract the adults.

Amari smiled. She would never forget the kindhearted woman who had befriended her.

Elbowing to a sitting position, she touched her scalp near her hairline. Her head wound was healed.

Pushing to her feet, she slipped behind a curtain and stripped out of her clothes. Running her fingers around her neck, she frowned and flattened her palm against her throat. The necklace was gone. Her only link to her past, lost.

She blinked away tears and stepped to a wash basin. Refusing to waste the precious time she had left dwelling on something she couldn't change, she rinsed off and slipped into a clean dress. After tying a braided belt around her waist, she secured the dagger—her last possession—at her hip, then stepped around the screen.

Sousa still held court tucked in the middle of the crowd.

"Goodbye, my friend," she whispered, then stepped outside.

The suns had reached their peak. With several hours remaining before they dipped below the horizon, she had plenty of time to distance herself from the bloodied meadow. Seeking courage, she caressed her recently acquired blade and headed for the trees.

CHAPTER 16

DRAGON'S QUARRY

After finding Amari and the boy in the thicket, Jaxon had shadowed Amari the entire way back to camp, his dragon watching her with the focused intensity of a predator studying its prey. Gavin had pushed out ahead, and Crispin had disappeared into the trees, flanking them from the right to put her in a protected position with him behind and to the left. The boy had stayed glued to Amari's side.

Jaxon's need to ensure her wellbeing pulsed strongly within him. So, when she disappeared into a healing tent after returning the boy to his mother, his beast demanded they check on her. Although a powerful healer in his own right because he could draw upon the strength of his dragon, confusion kept him from following her. Sheep and dragons couldn't be a more opposite species.

A memory rippled across his mind. His healing energy had automatically ignited when he'd assisted her out of the bramble. Although she had pulled away, his power had already delved deep into his reservoir, preparing for an extensive session. As he reflected, her uneven gait and measured steps back to camp indicated she favored one side.

Sousa, the elderly sheep shifter they acquired at auction, claimed to be an excellent medicine woman. While herbivores preferred healers of their same designation, he would ensure Amari's health if Sousa couldn't manage. Whether Amari accepted his offer or not, didn't matter. He thought her lost to him once, and refused to entertain the possibility of losing her again because of her discomfort over a predator tending her wounds.

His lips quirked. He almost wished the herb healer couldn't make Amari well so he'd have an excuse to touch her.

Gavin stepped out of the smaller tent and strode toward him. From Gavin's taut build, Jaxon recognized him as a worthy ally...or a formidable foe. Even his beast admired Gavin's fierceness, but the man waffling on his feet in front of him contradicted the warrior's self-assured demeanor and triggered his dragon's insatiable curiosity. "How is your arm?"

Gavin flexed his bicep. "Good as new. My thanks."

"Think nothing of it," Jaxon said while raising his hand in a dismissive gesture.

Gavin nodded, then glanced toward the healing tent. "Checking on your sheep?"

Jaxon arched an eyebrow, Amari being called his for the second time not going unnoticed. Even his beast approved. "Something seemed off with her. My dragon is concerned."

Smooth, blame it on my animal.

Gavin dragged his fingers through his dark hair. "She is different, that's for sure."

He noticed the leather sheath in the panther's hand. "For Amari?"

Gavin's mouth curved in a slight smile. "If she's going to carry my twin's blade, she should have a proper cover for it."

His dragon sniffed the panther. Was Gavin interested in her? A possessive seed sprouted in Jaxon's chest, which he promptly doused. They couldn't be interested in a sheep.

But she doesn't act like one, his beast protested.

For the love of the goddesses, they ate sheep for dinner!

She would taste sweet, his dragon agreed, then smacked its lips for emphasis.

Jaxon sighed. Could he really be attracted to an herbivore? As he remembered the swell of her breasts against her dress, his cock seemed to think so. Between his lecherous body and his beast's eagerness to mount her, he didn't stand a chance and needed to extricate himself from the situation.

"Crispin and I will be leaving soon. I'll bid my farewells to Lady Amari before talking to Nicula," he said, and almost doubled over when his dragon kicked him in the gut.

"Then I wish you safe journey." Gavin dipped his head and strode away.

Sousa swept out of the tent just as Jaxon approached. She spotted him, and her eyes clouded.

He nodded in greeting. "Amari came here earlier. I'd like to speak to her."

The woman glanced around.

His dragon leaned forward. Both he and his animal hated surprises. "I don't wish to disturb your patients, but I must speak to Amari before we leave."

The healer wrung her hands. "I'm sorry, Lord Blackthorn."

He frowned. "I understand the other shifters might be uncomfortable if I go inside, so she can come out here."

Sousa shook her head. "I cannot help you."

His beast postured. Anyone wishing to live a long life, especially an herbivore, did not want to irritate his crusty dragon.

From her grimace, Sousa realized her precarious situation.

"I'm not here to cause trouble. I only want to ensure Amari is well."

His dragon clawed his insides, insisting they walk past the old woman and go inside. Contrary to his ornery beast, he respected his elders, regardless of their designation, although even Jaxon had his limits.

"She's not here, my lord."

Unease knotted his stomach. "My apologies. Where might I find her?"

Sousa looked behind him toward the forest.

He followed her gaze, and his chest tightened. His dragon stepped to the forefront. "Where is she?" he demanded, his voice dropping an octave.

"Gone."

"Where?"

Sousa fixed him with a hard glare, displaying an unusual rod of steel for an herbivore spine. "Both of us know she's no sheep, my lord."

His eyes widened. Hearing Sousa say it out loud confirmed what he had innately known all along. Of course, Amari wasn't an herbivore. Only a predator would attract both him and his beast. Anticipation filled him, but the healer kept talking.

"When herbivores are about to pass over, they want to surround themselves with their friends and family. Predators, however, often prefer to face the end alone."

A low buzzing filled his ears. "What are you saying?"

"She's dying."

His dragon stilled. "What?"

Tears filled Sousa's eyes. "If I had known about her injuries when I first met her, I might have been able to save her."

Jaxon could barely contain his panicked beast. "Where did she go?"

Sousa waved her arm toward the forest. "Out there."

Fear wrapped around his gut and squeezed. "How long?"

"Two hours at the most."

He turned and sprinted toward the forest. Once clear of the tents, he released his raging dragon. In a surge of energy, he stepped aside so his animal could take over. His beast's wingtips skimmed the ground in powerful sweeps before propelling them up and over the treetops.

"Jax?" Crispin's voice entered his mind.

"Amari is missing. I'm going to find her."

Crispin's concern spilled across their link. *"I'll help you."*

"No. Stay and assist Nicula. Once I find her, we'll meet at the crossroads. If you arrive first, set up camp and wait for us."

"Very well. Safe journey."

****

Amari's initial trail proved hard to locate. More than once, he shifted back into man so he could search the forest on foot. As if the woodlands considered her a prize, her scent eluded him. He would start in one direction, only to backtrack and go in another. His latest track led him west. The suns' rays illuminated the land in a golden glow. The yellow orbs rode low in the sky and would soon succumb to the pull of the moons.

He had been searching for over three hours. Tension inhibited his ability to focus. Although his dragon wanted to eat Sousa for failing Amari, he couldn't condemn the healer. Essentially, he had done the same thing by not recognizing her injuries when his healing power activated.

He soared over the treetops, scanning for the smallest sign. His little shifter might have escaped him, but he would be damned if he was going to let her die. About to retrace his path, yet again, he almost didn't notice the scrap of cloth beside a narrow stream winding through a meadow.

Tucking his wings, he dove and transformed into a man an instant before his feet touched the ground. He grabbed the material and brought it to his nose. Amari's spicy scent filled his nostrils. Hope lightened his heart as he jumped into the air. His dragon pushed through a headwind, both vowing to have their sheep-that-really-wasn't-a-sheep in their grasp before sunset.

CHAPTER 17

CAUGHT

Amari followed an animal trail beside the brook, regretting her spontaneous decision to leave camp. The ache in her chest confirmed her poor choice. She would have liked seeing Lord Blackthorn one last time, if only to burn his image into her mind for her dreams.

Not sure where to go, she had walked toward the suns. At first, the rays dusted her in warmth until Sousa's pain inhibitors weakened and the sunbeams no longer offered comfort, but beat down on her with an unforgiving intensity.

Her dress caught on every twig and branch, and while attempting to muster the strength to step over a log, her foot snagged the hem and she toppled head first to the ground. Lying on the damp earth, she wallowed in her misery. She would die, never knowing who she was, or if she had a family. The suns were low in the sky when she finally sat up and pulled the dagger from her waistband.

She hated dresses. Although she might not remember anything about her past, she knew—without a doubt—she'd always despised them. Poking a hole in the material just below her knee, she slashed off the bottom portion. Once free from the entangling cloth, she dropped her mouth to the water and drank her fill, then topped off her water pouch and ate one of the three hard rolls she had taken from camp before pushing to her feet.

****

She didn't know how far she'd walked since the stream, but everything Sousa had done to lessen the pain had long worn off. Each step pounded through her body, and from the alternating sweats and chills, a fever had decided to join the party. Like a slow-moving fog, her mind fuzzed over and her concentration waned.

Shadows deepened beneath the canopy of trees. Although a gentle breeze cooled her overheated skin, the temperature wasn't the reason the hair on the back of her neck prickled. She surveyed the thickening gloom. Nothing stirred. Only her labored breaths and footfalls disturbed the stillness.

She angled toward a meadow and slid down a small ridge marking the forest edge. Tall, reedy stalks slapped at her legs, yet she kept her focus on the no-longer simple task of placing one foot in front of the other. Halfway across the field, she stopped. Her pulse thumped in her ears from pushing her body beyond its limits, but even her ragged rhythm couldn't mask the faint rustle in the air. She glanced behind her as goose bumps rose on her arms.

The silent meadow and surrounding trees screamed at her in warning. Her mind shuffled through the possibilities of who—or what—could be following her. She tilted her head and closed her eyes, listening. Her heart plummeted into her stomach over the deep sweep of wings slicing through the air.

Swoosh, swoosh, swoosh.

She crouched in the swaying blades and scanned the sky. The second sun had dropped below the trees, shooting spirals of light through the branches. Although darkness approached, aside from a few wispy clouds, the heavens remained clear and devoid of life.

Swoosh, swoosh, swoosh.

Tension knotted her shoulders. The beast would have to be large for her to hear it from a distance. She glanced at the path of bent stalks behind her telegraphing her location, then stood and forced her tired body into a jog toward the opposite side of the meadow.

Swoosh, swoosh, swoosh.

Closer. Ever closer. She resisted the urge to look over her shoulder as every impulse inside her screamed for expediency. Her labored pants blended with the powerful wing beats. The beast had reached the meadow.

Run!

A shadow loomed above her. Stifling a scream, she ignored the grass blades cutting into her flesh and kicked into high gear. Air blasted down on her from enormous wings. She would never make it. The shadow above her receded, but she continued running.

"Amari. Stop."

Although his voice caressed her like a lover's touch, her terrorized mind urged immediate flight instead of analyzing who called her. Unable to sustain her pace, her strides faltered. She stumbled and cried out. Black spots danced across her vision.

The beast grabbed her arm.

Thinking only of escape, she pulled her dagger.

Surprise flitted across his face an instant before he dodged her attack, receiving a glancing blow. He grabbed her wrist and wrenched the blade from her hand.

Madness clouded her brain. She punched his chest and scratched his face.

His arms banded around her, and her body erupted in pain before blessed nothingness sucked her into oblivion.

CHAPTER 18

THREATS

Greyson stood on the balcony, just one of many adorning his mountain fortress, unafraid that only empty space stood between him and a free fall over the side since no rail bordered the terrace. A chilly breeze soothed his dragon, but soon his beast would be pushing against him for the injustice of losing their eldest.

He had mated Selena with the belief they would never conceive, yet even years later, Amari's strength and beauty still amazed him. His family ruled his heart and soul, and he'd search to the end of the world and beyond to find any one of them.

When the plague killed most of the drakaina, he never intended on falling in love. Selena had been an unexpected deviation from his plan. The headstrong young Eldian noble had come out of nowhere and bewitched his dragon...and the man.

After their joining, both he and his beast yearned to return to the rugged wilds of their homeland, but Selena's kind heart again interfered with his intentions. She didn't want to leave her father alone after her mother's recent death. Seeing the pain in his mate's eyes messed with his resolve. So, to ensure her happiness, Greyson abandoned his lands to live within the confines of the veil.

A reminiscent smile touched his lips. He might be an alpha in every other aspect, but she ruled his nest. While he never expected his cadre to join him, they settled into their new home without reservation and embraced Selena as his bonded mate...like a true drakaina.

Greyson's dragon sat very still, perched on the edge, watching the Eldian village below. Nestled within the trees and spilling into the narrow valley that abutted his mountain, the hamlet hummed with afternoon activity. Originally a woodland folk, many Eldians still built their homes in the treetops of ancient oaks, using sweeping bridges to interconnect the dwellings in a latticework of passageways.

But, to Greyson's amusement, a growing number of young Eldians chose a more grounded home consisting of elegant marble structures with large round windows. Regardless of their age, all Eldians shared an intimate connection with the trees, each feeding off the other in a symbiotic relationship he didn't understand, but respected.

Selena's father, Teagen, never believed he and his cadre could exist within Evenglade's peaceful confines. Teagen had underestimated his beast...and their love for Selena. Although Selena's father had been correct in assuming dragons could never live within the trees, the stark mountain beside the village proved the perfect location for a dragon nest, a nest he would never abandon without his mate and family.

As if hearing his thoughts, Teagen swept into the receiving room with the air of a nobleman. "Any news?"

He inhaled a deep breath and turned away from the wind to face his father-in-law.

Teagen's silk robes bespoke of the man's council status, the diamond-embedded chips catching the light. Long silver hair flowed midway down his back, and small braids, interwoven with chimes, rested on each side of his head. The usually impeccably dressed man seemed a little rough this morning.

"Nolan and Bastaine are tracking her. Apparently, a trader sold her into servitude."

Teagen's gray eyebrows shot up. "But she's Eldian!"

Greyson folded his arms across his chest to contain the dragon his father-in-law unknowingly stirred.

"Trackers have no morals. They have been known to steal the helpless, then ensure their silence by threatening to kill loved ones. Amari's heritage wouldn't matter if she had no choice."

Teagen's sky blue eyes hardened. "When you find her kidnappers, I expect swift justice."

Although peaceful by nature, Eldians were fierce warriors. If threatened, they protected their children with a savagery even Greyson's dragon admired. While Greyson appreciated the love Teagen lavished on his children, telling him how to handle a threat to his nest irritated his already volatile beast.

"While I welcome the opportunity to rend justice on my daughter's behalf, your eagerness for my dragon's appearance is a bit two-faced."

Teagen waved his hand in dismissal. "To ensure peace, we agreed years ago that only a few select council members would know your true identity. Your girls blend into our culture free from teasing and bigotry." Teagen tilted his head and regarded him with a wary gaze. "Why do you question this arrangement now?"

Greyson kept his voice low, even though his beast had started pacing again. "Trinity approaches. Selena believes we should have told Amari what lives within her when she was young, and I do too."

"What then? She would've been different. Eldian children would have distrusted her." Teagen shook his head, jingling the small bells in his hair. "This discussion is a moot point anyway, because she would never survive transition as a half breed. You agreed to live within the veil so your children wouldn't experience Trinity and to ensure their safety."

Out of respect for his mate, Greyson didn't scorch Teagen to ash. "Amari isn't inside the veil, *is* she? If she knew about her animal, she would know her time is limited. She doesn't even realize this is her transition year." Greyson's voice dropped, his dragon pushing for release. "I think you underestimate your people and their willingness to accept us. Maybe it's time they decided for themselves."

Teagen stepped near the ledge beside him and clasped his hands behind his back, his arms disappearing within the folds of his robes. "My people are long-lived. They remember the bloodshed caused by your kind."

"A few dragons, distraught over losing their mates, and who erroneously believed Eldians created the plague to ensure the demise of our kind, cannot dictate the actions of the rest of us."

"Those few slaughtered hundreds of Eldians." Teagen threw him a sidelong glance. "Another elder spotted Nolan flying inside the veil a few days ago."

"Nolan was delivering an update."

"He can path you."

Greyson's jaw clenched. "He was here for Selena's benefit, not mine."

Teagen sighed and held up his hand in truce. "How is my daughter?"

While his father-in-law might be a thorn in Greyson's side at times, Teagen's devotion for Selena and the girls went unquestioned. "She fears for Amari, but is hopeful."

"And my unborn grandbaby?"

"Strong and safe."

Teagen's shoulders straightened. "We must keep them all safe."

"We will."

Like Eldians, dragon-born also were a family-oriented species. Nestlings were cherished. Although dragons could be patient, once Greyson's beast discovered who took Amari, it would show no mercy.

Teagen turned to leave. "Tell Nolan no more flying inside the veil."

"I'll relay the message."

CHAPTER 19

HEALING

Amari clawed his cheek before Jaxon could restrain her. Her body burned with fever. Lost in her delirium, his encouraging words went unheard. Jaxon's dragon raged, demanding he heal her. "I will," he muttered out loud as he laid her on a bed of leaves.

His power flared with a warming glow, and he touched her body, feeding her his energy while searching for her injuries. He grunted when he located the web the sheep elder spun to mend Amari's head trauma. Although the weaves held an herbivore signature, the strength anchoring the threads would ensure Amari healed completely. His dragon chuffed in appreciation over Sousa's ability.

Scanning downward, he reached Amari's abdomen and cursed aloud. Blunt trauma had lacerated her liver. Although any healer could have repaired the initial damage, left unattended, the bleeding had compressed major organs and was slowly suffocating her. Sousa's web sparkled around the edges of Amari's injured tissues. Gratitude softened his heart. Even though Sousa didn't have the power to repair Amari, she had bought him time. The old woman had just garnered a powerful predator as an ally.

As a man, Jaxon didn't have the strength to heal Amari either. Only his beast had the power. Although dragons were selfish creatures and hoarded the gifts the goddesses bestowed upon them, they were also fiercely loyal and protected what they cherished. With the extent of Amari's injuries, his beast would have to expend a tremendous amount of energy, which would make them vulnerable. Since Amari wasn't drakaina, another dragon with the healing ability might not have assisted, but Amari's willful nature had enamored his stodgy beast, and his dragon wasn't ready to let her go. Jaxon wasn't ready to let her go either.

Power flooded Jaxon's body, searing a path down his arm. He pressed his palm to Amari's abdomen, and she cried out. Her wail shot through him like a broad head spear.

"Shhh, sweet one."

She continued struggling until he finally straddled her hips to control her. She pushed against his chest, but he ignored her meager attempts to dislodge him.

Her teeth chattered as his energy dove deep inside her.

"St-*op*," she stuttered.

Her face contorted in pain, and his dragon wailed over the additional discomfort he inflicted to knit the organs and redirect her blood. "I'm sorry, *mon est draco*," my little dragon, he murmured in an ancient tongue, "but I must do this to make you well."

He pried her fingers off his shirt and interlaced them within his own. "Use me as your anchor, *nuri*." Young one. "I won't let you go."

She whimpered, but her grip tightened.

Sweat dotted his forehead from the power coursing through him, yet her energy still faded. She slipped into shock, and her fingers slackened in his hand.

No, no, no!

Although under normal circumstances, his dragon would have considered connecting with a shifter from a different designation repulsive, his beast demanded that Jaxon shed his physical self and enter her on a mental plane.

Her heart stumbled, and though he worked quickly, she would die of shock if he didn't tie her to him mentally. The delicate sweep of her dark lashes contrasted with her ashen skin and pale lips. Determination fortified his decision. He didn't need any encouragement from his animal because he too had no intention of losing her.

"You are mine," he ground out.

Even though his declaration surprised him, his beast accepted the decree with the conviction of an animal that lived...and loved...in absolutes. Once decided, his dragon would never stray or falter—and his animal had chosen Amari. Jaxon would have to analyze his possessiveness for the little shifter later, but until then, he disengaged his shields and entered her mind.

She immediately fled deeper inside herself, slamming up walls as she retreated.

He smiled over her attempts to elude him, but she didn't stand a chance against a seasoned alpha with over a century to hone his skill. Battle hardened and eager for the challenge, he dogged her with the stubborn tenacity of one used to getting his way.

With each wall she threw up, he unraveled the weaves and passed through. Like a surgeon, he worked with rapid efficiency, but remained gentle to avoid traumatizing her.

She reached her final grand barrier and backed against it before weaving one last shield. Although her beast resided on the other side of her grand barrier, she had chosen to throw up another shield to block him instead of unleashing her animal to attack him on a mental plane.

Anxiety crawled through him. He had her trapped. She couldn't escape, so expending her last bit of strength didn't make sense. Her makeshift shield pulsated in vibrant hues. Barriers usually throbbed in one dominant shade. He had never seen one with different colored ropes.

She bolstered her wall with each thread he unraveled, adding to the complexity of the weaves. For someone so young, her complicated knots and tightly woven plaits reminded him of an elder's touch, except she still lacked the fluidity to keep the barrier impenetrable. Although he admired her budding skill, the energy she consumed was taking a toll on her body.

Her heart stopped, forcing him to channel power to keep it beating. Her lungs collapsed, and he split his healing wave to inflate her airways.

"Nuri, let me help you."

Her fear confused him. His touch pulsed in the bright blue light of a healer. She should recognize the cerulean shade of his curative power. But instead, she acted as though she feared such a connection.

From birth, mental touches were commonplace among shifters. Parents offered love and spiritual nourishment through a familial linking. Additional bonds formed with close friends during teen and adult years. As alpha, he had a strong mental connection with his cadre. So to find her afraid of internal touch baffled him.

"Who are you, nuri, and what hides inside you?"

He studied the wall of energy and his chest tightened like a boa constrictor curling around his lungs. He'd never reach her in time by remaining gentle, but forcing entry would be akin to raping her mind. Although he'd then be able to heal her body, the brutal act of ripping through her shield would most likely destroy her emotionally. If she somehow remained intact, she would always associate his signature with an involuntary breach. Since he planned to someday touch every part of her intimately, he didn't want her recoiling whenever he reached for her.

Dragons could be very charming when the need arose. Jaxon's beast was no exception. Although not an innate charmer like Kip's animal, his could still lure the most hesitant female if it wanted—and with Amari, his dragon definitely wanted. To alleviate her fear, he dampened his energy and infused his need to help her within his whispered reassurances.

In a rare move, he dropped his inner shields. He had never offered such a deep link because the closeness exposed him to a mental attack. They would be irrevocably connected, tied on a most intimate level, if she accepted. Although he feared such a binding, hope fueled a nervous anticipation she would accept his offer.

He remained still, murmuring an epic tale about honor and battle just so she would hear his voice. Soon, a warrior's love sonnet spilled from his lips, and his dragon pitched in by crooning a lullaby his mother sang to him as a nestling.

Her barrier faded. He wooed her, encouraging her to relax so he could tend to her. The pulsating ropes thinned to a translucent film, and he gasped. He had been in many minds, either to heal or rip apart, but he had never seen such a brilliant energy signature. His eyes watered at her luminescence, both man and dragon in awe of her splendor. She reached for him in a tentative brush of someone untrained, yet her touch slammed through him like a thunderbolt. His body trembled, eager for her to graze his senses again.

His beast recovered first, excited to scramble across the barrier and claim her. Jaxon showed more restraint. She needed to entrust herself to his care. Although powerful, he already supported her heart and lungs, and his energy waned. Unless she submitted so he could focus all his attention on her injuries, he didn't know how much longer he could sustain her.

He rose so she could see his strength.

She shrank away, her shield gaining substance.

He murmured her name, enjoying the way it played off his tongue and sounded in his mind.

Her shield pulsed, yet she didn't reestablish the thick weaves to keep him out. Raising his hand, he eased through the barrier.

Although she cowered in a corner of her mind, he admired her courage...and beauty. Two more steps and he stood before her, her gold signature calling to him on a primal level. Dropping onto his haunches, he stared at her with the open-mouthed wonder of a nestling. His dragon urged him to take her, but he sensed her power. If she didn't agree to his touch, she would burn herself out fighting him.

She rested against her final barrier, her animal hidden behind that last throbbing wall. While he itched to discover her beast, he would save that encounter for another time. Extending his arm, he registered her fear...and curiosity. *"Come to me, nuri. No harm will befall you."*

She trembled with indecision while his beast begged for him to just grab her. He waited, holding out his hand. When she finally reached for him, her energy splashed across his senses in intoxicating bursts of sensation he absorbed like a starving man.

Finally, he allowed his dragon some freedom and drew her into his arms, soothing her with the patience of one who had lived a long and lonely life. Rubbing her back in calming strokes, he brushed his lips against her ear.

A final shudder rumbled through her before she relinquished herself to him. He tightened his arms around her and filled his lungs with her cinnamon scent. His dragon roared in triumph. Even though she didn't allow their energies to blend completely, she trusted him enough to succumb to his dominant power by creating a fragile link between them. He would nurture that bond, help it grow. Because now that he had touched her mind, he would never let her go. With her scent forever burned in his psyche, he closed his eyes and concentrated on her wounds.

"I'll take care of you, mon est draco...always," he promised, then nudged her into a deep sleep.

She collapsed in his arms, displaying the trust of a someday lover and mate.

CHAPTER 20

REFLECTIONS

Bringing Amari back from the brink of death was the hardest thing Jaxon had ever done. At one point, his energy signature was so thin, it barely registered. But since both he and his beast refused to let her die, he stubbornly denied his own exhaustion. Confusion clouded his mind. Although she hadn't merged with him entirely, if she had requested it, he would have willingly joined with her. Such a deep bond was usually reserved for mated pairs.

Why would I have done such a thing?

He stayed inside her body for hours. Once stabilized, he released her from the deep sleep so her mind could waken. Now that her initial fear was gone, she watched his every move as he healed her from within with the curiosity of one who had never witnessed someone shadow her mentally before.

Although an odd sense of pride filled his chest over being her first in establishing such an intimate contact, her innocence baffled him. The fact he couldn't sense Amari's animal added to the conundrum. She had to be close to her Trinity year, so her animal should be near the surface of her psyche. Yet, only Amari's essence surrounded him. Could she be a non-shifter? A one-soul? If so, what hid behind her grand barrier? And why would she place herself into servitude under a sheep designation?

Since the danger of losing her was gone, he released her mentally and withdrew from her mind so he could relish her sleeping beside him. Even his beast, who also watched over her, did not understand the pull she held over them. He wrapped an arm around her waist, but she refused to nestle at his side. Instead, she pushed onto his shoulder and draped an arm across his chest like she owned him. He marveled at her trust. Even in sleep, she should have realized the danger of lying with an alpha predator. Her breaths lengthened into deep slumber. Only another predator, a very powerful one, would feel comfortable enough to relax...on top of him.

She was a puzzle, taunting him with secrets buried deep inside her. Since both he and his animal loved riddles, he accepted her challenge.

As sleep pulled him under, he vowed to uncover the true identity of the beautiful woman who might have somehow captured a piece of his lonely heart.

CHAPTER 21

UNWISE CHOICES

Amari awoke to birds chattering above her. A gentle breeze cooled her skin and rustled the leaves overhead. She kept her eyes closed and concentrated on her surroundings. Her body hummed in awareness. She hadn't slept so soundly in days.

She lay on her side, her head resting in the crook of a shoulder with a muscled arm wrapped around her. Tilting her head, she spied her pillow and stifled a small gasp. Delicious, charcoal lashes rested against Lord Blackthorn's face. Lavish cheekbones tapered to a strong jaw. Her gaze drifted to his mouth, and wicked thoughts filled her mind. She resisted the urge to brush the stray strands of hair off his face and trace her fingers across his bottom lip. Cocooned within his embrace, peace infused her. Instead of being self-conscious for sleeping beside a man she hardly knew, her body tingled with excitement.

For the first time in days, she reveled in the absence of pain. Lord Blackthorn had spoken true. Her brows drew together. Although the events of last night were hazy, she did remember being chased across a meadow, but everything else seemed like a dream.

He had entered her mind, a larger than life impression of the man, offering words of encouragement and promises to heal. His mental energy then latched onto her in an intoxicating showcase of power that sucked the air from her lungs, only to be replaced with his own. She had basked in his aura, immersing herself within it to the point she almost accepted the bond he had offered.

She exhaled a frustrated breath. Why did her body burn for this man? She mulled over waking him, but dark circles camped beneath his eyes. She inched free of his arm and crouched beside him. Her gaze drifted across his massive chest, downward, to the bulge in his pants, and her cheeks flushed with heat. Her fingers twitched and she reached for him. She would be so careful, he'd never feel her touch—

Flames!

She snatched her hand back and clutched it to her chest as if she had just been scalded with hot water.

Shaking her head, she pushed the sordid thoughts from her mind. Had she actually contemplated waking a sleeping dragon?

Silly girl.

Stewing in disappointment over her lack of courage, she stood and glanced around. Lord Blackthorn had sequestered them inside a shallow cave. Peeking through the bushes hiding their sleeping place, she spotted the meadow glittering in the morning light. Instead of the open field, she skirted their makeshift shelter and padded deeper into the forest.

She supposed the woods should intimidate her, a lone female in a potentially hostile environment, but instead, the confining oaks comforted her. Sunbeams filtered through the branches as the suns claimed the day on their journey upward. A squirrel scolded her for coming too close to its den before scampering underground. She smiled over the little creature's brazenness. Insects buzzed and birds sang. With her body healed, she could fully appreciate the tranquility of her surroundings.

Worming her way into a thicket, she relieved herself, then followed the babbling sound of water to a small stream, where she rinsed and washed her face. Inhaling a deep breath, she marveled over the easy expansion of her ribs. A flat rock beckoned her to sit, and she complied, tilting her face skyward to bathe in the sun like a lizard.

Lord Blackthorn had done the impossible. She owed him a huge debt, but how did one thank a dragon lord?

Sudden snarling and a high-pitched squeal shattered the quiet. Shifting onto her haunches, she focused on the opposite bank, ready to bolt if the ruckus spilled from the trees. A growl, followed by a thump, rattled the bushes.

The crack of snapping branches, then a roar spurred a tingling down her spine. Instead of returning to the man who would protect her, she jumped up and crossed the stream, pondering her impulsiveness. Not only couldn't she remember, but she didn't appear very smart either.

She leapt onto the damp bank. Muffled snarls and muted bleats drifted from the trees. Her feet sank into the loamy soil as she stepped forward.

She had lost her mind.

That seemed the only logical explanation for the inexplicable urge to witness what would most likely result in a predator killing its prey. Regardless of her madness, nervous anticipation propelled her deeper into the woods. She scurried over fallen logs and around trunks until the trees thinned. Her pulse quickened as she edged closer to the sounds of snapping jaws, stamping hooves, and snorting breaths.

Stopping at an outcropping of boulders, she tilted her head and listened. The hair on her arms rose over the life-and-death confrontation unfolding on the other side. Her hand settled on the stone and she looked up. She'd have a bird's-eye view if she climbed to the top.

Resting her foot against the rocks, she pushed herself up. The rough stone scraped her hands as she leveraged herself higher. Although her limbs trembled by the time she scrambled to the top, she smiled over her accomplishment. Pausing to catch her breath, she thanked Lord Blackthorn again for healing her. A loud *crack* startled her, but the resulting scream had her diving to her belly.

Inching forward, she peered over the edge, and her eyes widened.

A mountain lioness crouched a few feet away from a mother reindeer and her small calf. The reindeer lowered her antlered head and pawed the ground. Undaunted by the herbivore's posturing, the lioness lunged. The reindeer bellowed and used her rack as a battering ram to repel the cat.

Amari had overheard an herbivore shifter mention that two-souls couldn't transition into their animal until their twenty-third year, so based on the baby reindeer's presence, the animals below had to be true beasts. Although she respected the mother reindeer for guarding her young, the muscled fluidity of the cat drew her attention. The lioness hugged the ground, motionless, except for the twitch of her tufted tail. Scars marred her body, but even with the blemishes, Amari admired the cat's strength.

Rising to her knees, she grabbed a fist-sized stone, then stood.

The cat spotted her and snarled.

"Go," she commanded and threw the rock. The stone hit the ground and bounced twice before hitting the cat's flank.

The cat leapt away, but kept the panicked mother and calf pinned against the boulders.

Amari shooed the lioness with her arms. "Leave them alone!"

The cat flattened its ears and settled in the grass.

She threw another rock, pelting it on the shoulder. When the cat barely flinched, another piece of Amari's past clicked into place.

She did not like being ignored.

Another stone flew from her hand, then another...and still another until sweat trickled down between her shoulder blades. She grabbed two more rocks and raised her arm. Hesitating only a moment, she hurtled the projectiles forward. Her momentum threw her off balance, and she slipped. In a flurry of falling gravel, she tumbled off her sanctuary and landed on the hard ground below with a painful *thud*. Small stones and dirt rained down on her, and she raised her arms to shield herself.

Her sudden appearance proved too much for the reindeer. The mother squealed and bolted with her calf at her heels. When the dirt settled and the spatter of pebbles eased, she dropped her arms. To her dismay, two yellow eyes stared back at her, and the very agitated lioness lifted its lip in a snarl.

So...things hadn't gone quite as planned.

Amari pulled her dagger and held it in front of her.

The cat stalked her, bending the blades of grass in that fluid motion only a predator could achieve. She crouched, her heart pounding against her ribs. When the lioness charged, she would deflect with her right arm and plunge her blade into its chest. "Go!" she yelled, but her show of force sounded more like a plea.

The cat's strides lengthened.

Her grip on the blade tightened.

The lioness lunged, and Amari shrieked.

A shadow blocked the sun, and a roar spilled from the heavens.

Startled, the cat twisted in mid-air and landed a few feet away.

Another earsplitting bellow from above rattled Amari's bones. She closed her eyes and clutched her ears. The ground shuddered beneath her feet as a large creature dropped down in the meadow behind her.

The cat's growl paled in comparison to the newly arrived creature's hiss, which pebbled her arms with goose bumps. Fire erupted beside her, the heat from the blast searing her skin. She cried out and crouched, throwing her arms over her head to protect herself. The lioness crashing through the brush in retreat barely registered in her ears as she willed herself into a tighter ball.

Maybe if she made herself small, she wouldn't appear worth eating.

The creature approached. Soft exhales ruffled her hair. She trembled and hunkered lower.

Go away. Please, go away.

A hard push against her shoulder knocked her onto her hands and knees, instigating a sort of snorting hiccup from the beast. She scrambled to her feet and turned around. Dread pooled in her belly. The blade she clutched would not protect her against this predator. Her mouth dropped open, but a scream never materialized.

An enormous dragon loomed above her, its black scales shining like oiled armor.

The creature folded its wings and lowered its head. Amber eyes glared at her.

Although her day had started out so well, somewhere along the way, it had taken a very bad turn. She had just wanted to enjoy a stroll in her healed body, yet had somehow become the main course for, not one, but two predators.

Well, *she* was hungry too. She raised her dagger. "Don't even think about eating me."

The dragon chuffed softly.

Was it...*laughing* at her? Her jaw clenched. "I mean it."

Additional snorts, then the beast leaned forward, and inhaled.

She stepped back, but it nudged her shoulder. "Stop that." She batted it away, which resulted in more of the odd chuffing sounds. Since the creature seemed only interested in playing with its food, she secured her blade and folded her arms.

She had never seen a dragon before...at least not from what she could remember. Muscle rolled beneath glistening scales. Front claws, consisting of sharp, black talons, shimmered like polished stone. Beautiful translucent wings rippled in the sunlight, tapering down to a powerful tail. Her body quivered over the breathtaking spectacle in front of her.

She skimmed her fingers over a large, amber eye, well away from the razor-sharp teeth. Aside from a slight twitch, the beast stilled at her touch. In a brazen move, she planted her palms on each side of its face. "You are way more magnificent than the lioness."

The dragon growled, shooting vibrations up her arms. She snatched her hands off its face and backpedaled until she butted up against the rock. Her heart rabbited in her chest.

She had just touched a dragon.

She glanced sideways. If she ran, maybe she'd reach the trees before it could catch her...assuming it wouldn't just torch her. As if reading her mind, the beast snarled.

"Please, don't eat me."

In a flash of light, the dragon shimmered and lost shape. To her surprise, Lord Blackthorn stepped from the brightness, and his hands slammed down on each side of her head, sandwiching her against the rock. Tension rolled off his shoulders, and fear crawled up her spine.

She almost preferred her chances with the dragon.

A muscle ticked in Blackthorn's jaw. Midnight eyes swirled like mini tornadoes, waiting for an excuse to unleash. "What in *flames* were you thinking?"

She gulped. "I...I don't know what you're talking about."

He leaned forward, his face inches from hers. "The mountain lioness? With only a dagger?"

Oh, right.

She pointed to the overhang. "I slipped."

His eyes narrowed. Disapproval marred his striking features. "Foolish girl."

She gasped. Anger replaced her fear; only *she* could call herself foolish. No doubt Lord Blackthorn was dangerous and probably controlled more by his beast. She should just apologize, but something inside her refused to yield.

She squared her shoulders and ground her teeth. "I was only trying to scare the lioness away...and don't call me foolish."

His nostrils flared, and with a final step, his body rested against hers. Her heart rate accelerated like a shooting star. He smelled of leather and musky beast.

He bent his elbows and rested along the stone with her body wedged between him and the rock face. "Why was the lioness less deserving?"

Her breasts tingled from his baritone rasp. She didn't know how to respond. Except for the lascivious images filling her brain, the logical portion of her mind had fled. She shook her head. "I don't understand—"

"The lioness." He captured a lock of her hair between his thumb and forefinger. "She's a nursing mother, and from her gaunt frame, probably hasn't eaten in days. Why were she and her offspring less deserving than the reindeer and calf?"

Amari's initial bravado crumbled. She had never considered the needs of the lioness. "I didn't think—"

"No, you didn't," he ground out. "And almost got yourself killed."

"I'll be more careful," she promised, wishing he would leave so she could clear her mind. His gaze heated her skin, and she squirmed, inadvertently rubbing against him. Warmth pooled in her belly.

He inhaled a sharp breath. A night's worth of stubble and disheveled hair enhanced his wildness. Instead of shying away, she longed to soothe his clenched jaw by brushing her thumb across his bottom lip.

Even now, with the danger gone, Jaxon's frustration over Amari's carelessness obliterated coherent thought. Inhaling deep breaths through his nose, he struggled to slow his racing heart. He had reached her in time...again. She was safe.

His alarm quickly morphed into anger, and he crowded her against the rock.

Her terror bled through their new link, and he grunted in satisfaction. At least she was smart enough to fear him. But then, something shifted inside her. The vibration echoed along their connection. She hadn't closed their link by resurrecting her shields after the healing session, which affirmed his belief that she was untrained in such communication.

A gentleman would have informed her of her vulnerability and voluntarily disconnected their link, but since she was only susceptible to his mental touch, he kept quiet, rationalizing he would be able to find her easier the next time she got into trouble. His dragon nodded in agreement, confirming they weren't noble creatures.

While he expected the defiance sparking in Amari's brilliant, green eyes, the flicker of heat took him by surprise. She licked her bottom lip and his gaze fixated on the moistened flesh.

He shook his head. He was a dragon lord, a predator. And she? Flames, he didn't know what in dragon spit she was, but regardless, he shouldn't care about her breasts pressed against his chest, or the subtle curve of her lips. And he definitely shouldn't be noticing her spicy scent mixed with the wonderful hint of arousal.

He dropped his hand to her nape, ensuring her capture. She quivered, although he no longer thought fear encouraged her reaction. His fingers trailed along her shoulder, then down to her waist. Splaying his hand wide at her lower back, he pulled her against his erection.

Her gasp shot straight to his groin. He shouldn't be acting this way. She was so young, barely out of the nest, and yet, his dragon...wanted her.

Protect. Claim.

His lips whispered along her neck. Opening his mind, he slipped inside the door she had left open...his door. Hiding in the shadows, he reached out to her. Fear thrummed along their connection. He understood fear...she *should* be afraid. Yet, he didn't expect curiosity, and combined with her arousal, his little sheep wannabe proved too irresistible to ignore.

He settled against her. Holding her waist, he reasserted dominance by wrapping his other hand behind her neck. Leaning close, he brushed his thumb against her jaw. "Are you afraid?"

"Yes," she answered in a throaty whisper.

"But I protected you from the lioness."

"Then almost ate me."

He chuckled low. "That I did. Still, I deserve a boon for saving you and then sparing you from my hungry dragon, don't you think?"

She stiffened. "What kind of boon?"

He smiled against her cheek. His dragon had her right where it wanted her. "A kiss."

The End, part one

SLEEPING DRAGON STIRS

PART TWO

CHAPTER 1 — FIRSTS

The dragon lord's hard body commandeered Amari's personal space as if he owned it, and her emotions took over, short-circuiting higher cognitive reasoning.

He was right; she was foolish. Instead of railing against him, she longed to explore the ridges and planes of his chest. Her body ached, stirring something inside her. Something she feared more than the dragon lord, whose hand currently perused her flesh with the arrogance of a man who took what he wanted. She acknowledged her true fear. *He* should be the one afraid, not her. Evil lived in the shadowy recesses of her mind. A darkness so buried in her subconscious, she didn't know what it was...or remember, anyway.

Lord Blackthorn encouraged that malevolence by urging her to succumb to the sensations coursing through her. Although she remained still under his touch, every particle inside her wanted to adhere itself to his body and never let go.

She couldn't explain her desire, she just wanted him to ease the hurt. While a kiss didn't seem like proper payment, he had saved her life...twice. Just a quick peck. How difficult could it be? If he kissed her, then maybe he would let her go, so she could step away and regroup.

His lips skimmed her jaw, shooting chills through her. "Are we in accord?"

Amari's knees wobbled. If she let go, she would drown within his husky tone. The rustle of his shirt teased her breasts with the promise of his touch. She shouldn't agree. Any sane female would run. Thankfully, since she'd already demonstrated she wasn't well-balanced, she nodded.

Thank you for purchasing *Rogue Dragon Rising*. If you enjoyed the first part of Jaxon and Amari's story, please consider leaving a review on a retailer or book review site.

Sleeping Dragon Stirs will be available for preorder in October, 2018.

For additional information about *Sleeping Dragon Stirs* and *Alpha Dragon Awakes*, sign up for TJ's newsletter on her website, https://tjshaw.com/. For signing up, TJ will send you the download link to the deleted prologue from *Rogue Dragon Rising*!

ABOUT TJ SHAW

As a child, TJ thrived in the Arizona desert. By the age of five she was riding horses through cotton fields, and by eleven, bought her first motorcycle. Growing up with teachers as parents meant traveling during the summer. Hiking, backpacking, fly fishing, climbing pyramids, surviving earthquakes, and flying in hot air balloons were just some of her adventures. An avid day dreamer, she would lose herself in mystical worlds and far off places limited only by her imagination.

Her debut novel, *Caller of Light,* a high fantasy romance, was dedicated to her mother who died of ovarian cancer. Following the success of *Caller*, she entered the realm of vampires and cops. Using her experience as a police officer and felony crimes prosecutor, she applied a realistic background to the paranormal world she created for *Divergent Bloodline*.

In *Rogue Dragon Rising* and the *Outside the Veil* series, TJ returns to her first love, high fantasy romance.

TJ writes from her heart by incorporating her dreams and experiences to create strong, passionate characters who must overcome personal flaws to survive against the challenges of traversing through magical realms, undiscovered planets, and apocalyptic catastrophes.

You may contact TJ at https://tjshaw.com/. She'd love to hear from you.